Blind Evil
Under the Breaking Sky 8
Copyright © 2023 Nick Clausen

Edited by Diana Cox
Cover by Deranged Doctor Design

The author asserts his moral rights to this work.
Please respect the hard work of the author.

To learn what is good, a thousand days are not sufficient.
To learn what is evil, an hour is too long.

1
CAMILLA

"Camilla!"

She blinks and comes to.

Mark is holding her shoulders firmly, looking her in the eye. They're still in Erika's apartment.

"You need to get that idea out of your head," he says. "No one is killing anyone. We're going down there, and we are going to talk to each other. We will figure it out. All right?"

Camilla blinks again. "All right, Mark. I hear you."

"Do you?" he asks, studying her eyes.

She's not sure how her face looks, but she believes she manages a smile. "Loud and clear."

Mark looks at her for a few more seconds. Then his expression softens, and he says, "Good. Let's go down there."

"Just, please ... Let me clean up a little."

Mark smiles. "You look fine."

"No," she says. "I look awful. It'll only be a minute."

She goes to the bathroom, closes the door, and sees herself in the mirror. She looks like someone who's terminally ill. She takes a clean cloth from the cabinet, drenches it in warm water, and washes her face. Then she finds a towel, and pauses for a moment to inhale the smell of fabric softener. It's mixed with something else. Something like smoke. As she looks back into the mirror, she understands why.

Allan is standing behind her, arms crossed, a lit cigarette hanging from his lips. The smoke rises up in front of his face, and he closes one eye, making it seem like he's winking at her. "Long time, no see."

"Fuck off," Camilla whispers. "You're the last thing I need to deal with right now."

"I'm not here to be dealt with, Camilla. I'm not the pushy type. Remember? I waited politely until you made the first move before I—"

"Shut up!" Camilla hisses, whirling around. She's very close to attacking him. Going for his face, clawing his eyes out. What holds her back is the fact that she knows he's not real, and interacting with him will only make the delusion stronger. "I'm not talking to you."

"I think that's clever," he says calmly as she heads for the door. "If you ask me, the time for talking is over. Too bad Mark doesn't agree, huh?"

Camilla wavers with her hand on the knob.

Go! her mind commands her. *Don't listen. Don't engage. Just leave!*

But she can't help it. She looks back at Allan.

Taking a deep drag off of the cigarette, he drops the butt and squishes it under his boot heel, leaving black stains on the expensive tiles. "I mean, that woman down there, if she has half a brain, she'll turn around and bolt the moment Mark spills the beans about what that guy who took Danny wants from you.

You really think she'll hang around people assigned to kill her? Would *you* do that?"

He finally looks at her, raising one eyebrow, sending her that signature bad boy look she still remembers. She realizes to her horror it's kind of attractive. Part of what she fell for in Mark—a big part, in fact—was exactly his bad boy attitude.

"That's right," Allan says, grinning, as though she just said something out loud. "Every damsel needs a bad boy now and then, whether they care to admit it or not. Someone who'll dig in and get their hands dirty. Do what's necessary." He throws out his arms. He's wearing a tight T-shirt under his vest, revealing his tanned biceps. "Hell, if I was here in flesh and blood, I'd happily do you the favor. I'd go down there and blow her brains out before she could say 'hello.' It'd be as easy as pie. We could even call it quits. I know I messed you up a little, what with the stuff I did to you and all, but helping you get your baby boy back, that'd make us even, wouldn't it?"

"It … would," Camilla hears herself say. The words are strained. As though they don't want to come out. But she's not in control of them. "Can you … can you do it?"

Allan smacks his lips. "Sorry, no. Like I said, I'm just a ghost, you know. Like Patrick Swayze. And just as sexy." He smiles again, and Camilla feels a shiver run down her back.

"I'm leaving," she says, turning towards the door.

"Yeah, you go," Allan says in a casual tone. "Probably for the best. Go to your pussy-ass boyfriend and let him do the talking. See if that gets you Danny back."

Camilla stops once more with her hand on the handle. She closes her eyes, and fresh tears begin spilling down her face.

"Look," Allan says, sighing. "I'm sorry about this crappy situation. I hope you know I didn't have anything to do with it. Right hand to God, I didn't. I'm just the guy who screwed you up as a child. I don't even know why I'm here. I'm not into stealing babies. Truth be told, I think it's despicable. That skinny dude ... Fritz, was it? ... he needs an ass-whooping, if you care to hear my opinion on the matter. Again, I would be happy to oblige, but ... anyway, as much of a coward as he is, I don't think you'll want to mess with him. I think he means business. Honestly, I don't even think he's above killing infants."

Camilla spins around to glare at him. "You stop talking, right now."

Allan holds up his hands as though she's pointing a gun at him. "Sorry, sexy, but I can't. You need to hear this. Because for all we know, that psycho could be pulling off Danny's tiny fingernails with a pair of pliers right now, and—"

"*Shut up! Shut uuup!*"

Camilla screams so loud, it hurts her own ears.

Allan stops talking. He just looks at her earnestly.

"*Camilla?*" Mark's voice through the door, full of concern. He grabs the handle, but the door is locked. Funny, Camilla doesn't remember locking it. "*Are you OK?*"

"I'm ... fine," Camilla says, not taking her eyes off of Allan. "It was just ... nothing."

Allan smirks. "That's not how I'd describe myself, but fair enough."

"Please, open the door, Camilla."

And she turns around to do just that, when Allan says in a calm, almost caring voice: "If he won't do it, you'll have to. There's no other way, Camilla. And you know it."

She hesitates another second, then she unlocks the door and opens it.

Mark comes in, looking her up and down, scanning the room. "What happened? Was it him? Allan?"

Camilla nods. No point in denying it.

Mark takes her by the arms. "What did he say?"

She inhales shakily. "Just the usual. Teasing me. Trying to get inside my head."

Why aren't you telling him the truth?

"I'm sorry," Mark says. "You've got enough on your plate already."

For some reason, the sincere sympathy and comfort she hears in his voice makes her angry. It's completely illogical. Part of her realizes it's her own stuff that's causing this. She's damaged goods; anyone willing to put up with a guy like Mark for years must be. Yet something made her stick with him, even through his affair with Erika. That something is the messed-up girl inside of her, the girl that got abused as a child, then lived with the burden in silence because she couldn't confide in the people who claimed to be responsible for her well-being. The girl that doesn't think she deserves a sensitive guy who truly cares for her. The girl that prefers a bad boy, a loose cannon, someone who's bound to let her down, because at least that's familiar and something she's able to deal with.

And now that she finally needs Mark to be that guy who's willing to break some moral rules, he's gone soft on her.

"Babe?" Mark asks, pulling her from her thoughts. "Are you sure you're OK?"

Camilla takes his hand. "Please promise me we'll get Danny back."

Mark kisses her hand. "I promise you. We'll get him back."

Camilla breaks into tears yet again. It seems like she's been crying nonstop ever since Alicia took Danny. She can't help it. She all but collapses in Mark's arms. He catches her and holds her tightly. They stand like that for half a minute, Camilla sobbing, Mark stroking her hair, telling her it'll be all right.

Then, finally, the tears subside. Camilla wipes her face in her already drenched sleeve.

"You ready?" Mark asks.

She nods.

"Great. Let's go see them."

He takes her right hand and leads her to the front door.

Good thing he didn't take her left hand, because then he would have felt the gun.

As they walk through the apartment together, Camilla slips the weapon into the back pocket of her jeans. It's a bit too big to go in all the way, but at least it doesn't fall out.

Mark unlocks the front door and steps out onto the landing. Camilla follows him, and she sees Allan standing there, leaning against the wall, busy lighting up another cigarette, acting like he doesn't even notice her.

Then, as they begin descending the stairs, Allan raises his hand to send her a thumbs-up along with a wide smile.

2
NORA

"It's too late ... I can't diffuse it ... No, please don't ... Make it stop!"

Nora wakes up, feeling immediately annoyed. This is the fifth time the boy pulls her out of sleep. He's in the bunk next to her, tossing and turning. He keeps muttering about something he needs to diffuse. He'll often call out for his dad to help him.

Nora glares at him. *For God's sake, just fucking sleep, will you?*

She sits up, running her hands through her hair. It's still dark, and all around them, people are snoring peacefully. She checks her watch. The hands and digits glow in the dark. It was a birthday gift from Nick, back when they both turned 20. She gave him a watch almost exactly like it. They hadn't spoken about it beforehand. It was one of those many, strange not-really-coincidences.

It's five thirty. Too early to get up—her shift in the kitchen doesn't start until seven forty-five—but there's no way she's going back to sleep now.

"But it'll blow up everything ... I have to stop it ..."

Tommy is still whispering, still whipping his head back and forth.

It's very normal, and Nora should be patient with him. Almost anyone who arrives here experience nightmares the first few days. Depending on the gravity of their trauma, it might even take weeks.

But eventually, whatever is plaguing their subconscious, it goes back down and stays there. When it happened to Nora, she felt relief. Nick was dead, and there was nothing she could do about it, so she preferred to simply forget the pain.

The boy seems to carry a particularly heavy burden. Of course she can't talk to him about it while he's awake, but from what Nora has gathered from his nightly murmuring, he built and set off some kind of bomb that killed several people. Which of course explains the name Fritz gave him.

Why Nora was tasked with taking care of him, she doesn't know. Perhaps she was simply the closest person when Fritz arrived with him. Either way, she hates it, and she looks forward to when he's finally able to handle things on his own. So far, Nora has pretty much been his personal caretaker. If she doesn't nudge him, he just sits there with a blank expression. She's the one who needs to bring him to the kitchen at meal times, fill his plate, instruct him to eat. She even takes him to the bathroom. And just yesterday, she started training him in the work he'll be doing: carrying supplies from the trucks.

Nora noticed the flow of new arrivals has finally stagnated. She was starting to wonder how they'd fit any more people into the sleeping barracks, but then Fritz stopped bringing them in. She's not sure how many they are altogether, but it's several hundred, if not thousands.

Nora doesn't feel particularly at home here. She does appreciate how the place is keeping the thoughts of Nick at bay. But she's not motivated to do the work, like so many others seem to be. It's almost like they found a purpose when they arrived here.

Perhaps it's because Nora still has unfinished business. And it's something she needs to keep secret. Because if anyone finds out what she's planning, she'll be immediately banned. Or worse; she might end up like the Bouncer. Fritz had the poor guy taken down yesterday, and only because crows kept flying into the hangar and picked away at the corpse, dropping pieces of flesh to the floor.

And yet, it's a risk Nora is willing to take.

She needs to.

For Nick.

The girl can't get away with what she did.

She's seen Nick several times now. Always in brief glimpses. He'll suddenly be standing next to her, watching her silently. As soon as she turns her head to look at him, he vanishes.

She knows why he's here, of course.

Nora stole a small paring knife from the kitchen along with two thick rubber bands. She now walks around with the knife secured to the outside of her left ankle, hidden by her pantleg. As soon as she gets the chance, she will use it to cut the girl's throat. Just like she cut Nick's.

But she needs to do it without getting caught, and that's the difficult part. She could have done it a dozen times by now, whenever they accidentally met during the days—it was hard to avoid, because the girl worked in the cleaning department, which was right next to the kitchen. Nora could have simply walked over to her, placed herself behind her, slipped out the knife, and gotten the job done.

But she much prefers getting away with it unnoticed. It's not the end of the world if they do catch her and she's killed—Nora doesn't really have much left to live for—but she doesn't want to be tortured first.

Besides, what's even a bigger threat is that if she's caught in the act but manages to escape, she can never return to the Palace. And that means she'll have to face all the pain and grief that the place helped her get successfully stuffed away deep down, out of sight.

So, there really is no question. The girl needs to die. But no one can know it was Nora who did it.

She got very close to doing it the day before yesterday. They met in the shower. Nora didn't notice the girl right away, because there were half a dozen other women showering as well. Then some of them finished up, and suddenly, it was just Nora, the girl, and a fat woman. That's when Nora and the girl finally noticed each other, and the girl quickly finished up and went to the dressing room.

Nora turned off the water, leaving the rest of the shampoo in her hair, in order to follow her.

They were alone in the dressing room. The girl was pulling on her clothes while still wet, obviously wanting to get away from Nora.

Nora went straight for her clothes. Sleeping and showering were the only two times she couldn't keep the knife on her, and so she tucked it away inside her shoe. Slipping it out, she hid it discreetly by her side, then went around the lockers and approached the girl. She had her back turned, and she'd just put on her bra. Now, she was pulling on her black shirt, but because her hair was still wet, it stuck, and she fumbled with it, more and more frantic.

Her side was completely exposed. Nora had envisioned slitting her throat a thousand times, but she would settle for plunging the knife into her liver.

Upping her speed, Nora's bare feet made no sounds on the tile floor, and her eyesight zoomed in on the soft spot right above the girl's hip.

When she was just two paces away, the door opened, and four women came in. Nora walked right by the girl, who didn't even notice her. She went back to her clothes, and with her heart pounding away in her chest, she hid the knife away, dried her body, got clothed and simply left the dressing room.

So close.

But she'll get another chance. She just needs to keep her eyes open. It's not like any of them are going anywhere. Sooner or later, they'll bump into each other with no one else around, and Nora will be ready for it.

3
GINA

"What's taking him so long?" Anton asks, shifting in his seat.

They're still in the back of the truck. It's idling in front of the door to number 118. Through the window, they can make out the building. It has a large canopy over the glass door, which could fairly easily be broken, but Gina sees no reason for it. It needs a combination to be unlocked, and Mark has that combination.

"I'm sure he'll be here any moment," she says.

"How do you know him again?" Lisa asks. She's clutching her dad's arm with one hand and stroking Rex's head with the other.

"We met briefly during the first incident," Gina says. "We were brought in for questioning together. It was your dad who did the interviews."

"Right. So you don't *know him*, know him?"

Gina shakes her head. "I know he's immune. And I believe he's freed himself of his ghost."

"But you don't know what he's like?"

"I'm sure we can trust him," John says, before Gina can answer. "And if we get the feeling we can't, we'll leave again. No harm done."

Lisa considers this for a moment. "Is he alone?"

"His girlfriend is with him. And their child. Apparently, she gave birth very recently."

"Oh." This seems to make Lisa slightly less anxious. Then, her expression turns dark again. "What a time to have a baby."

"Yes, it must be very—"

A knock on the window.

Nick points ahead.

Gina sees the figures behind the glass door. A young couple. She recognizes Mark, even though he's changed since they saw each other last. He's still wearing the leather jacket, but that's pretty much the only thing that hasn't changed. He's clean-shaven, newly washed, and his eyes are more alert. Not that Mark was a dull, inattentive guy before—in fact, he struck Gina as both sharp-witted and on-edge most of the time. But now, he seems more *there*.

He opens the door and steps out, squinting against the sunlight.

Behind him, his girlfriend stays right inside, peeking past Mark at the truck. Mark raises a hand in a greeting gesture.

Gina taps Nick on the shoulder and tells him to shut off the engine. "Let's get inside," she says to the others, "before any blind people show up."

John has already gone to the back and is opening the door, Lisa right on his heels. Gina jumps out, then helps Anton and Lisa down. John manages on his own. Gina has decided that, John being the classic strong guy type, self-reliant and proud, she'll only help him if he asks—and so far, he hasn't.

They go around to the front to meet up with Nick, who's standing next to the driver's side door. They all automatically step under the canopy, blocking the view of the sky.

Mark looks at Gina as they approach, pointing at Nick. "This guy doesn't talk?"

"No, he's deaf. His name is Nick. Nice to see you again, Mark."

Mark returns her polite smile. "Same." Then he looks at John. "Agent Nygaard."

John scoffs. "I'm no more an agent than you, Mark. This is my daughter Lisa. The boy is Gina's, his name is Anton."

"I've heard of you," Mark says, looking at Lisa. "Your dad mentioned you while we were being held by the government."

Lisa smiles briefly, then looks away.

Mark steps aside and looks back at the woman still waiting in the doorway. "Camilla? Won't you say hello?"

The woman takes a couple of steps forward. She's not holding the baby in her arms, as Gina expected. Maybe the little fellow is sleeping soundly back up in the apartment. Still, it seems a bit strange that a mother would leave her newborn out of sight, even for a minute. Especially these days.

"Hello," Camilla croaks, glancing around at them. "Nice to meet you all."

She both looks and sounds like someone who was recently crying; her eyes puffy, her voice raw.

"Where is your boy?" Gina asks, looking at Mark. "Didn't you say …?"

Mark sighs. "That's what we need to talk to you guys about. Come in, please."

He waves them closer, and John and Lisa move forward. Anton is about to do the same, but Gina grabs his arm, holding him back.

"What is it, Mom?" he asks, briefly awakening from the grief-induced stupor he's been in all day.

Gina is staring at Camilla, and Camilla is staring back at her. The moment their eyes met, it became instantly clear to her that Camilla is not only in deep distress, she's also about to do something drastic. It doesn't seem like Mark is in on it or even aware of it, because he's still looking at them, inviting them in with an earnest expression.

Camilla's hand goes to her back, and even before she's pulled out the gun, Gina has stepped in front of Anton, covering him.

Camilla begins breathing like someone who's been holding their breath for a long time as she points the weapon at Gina.

Lisa—who's the person nearest to Camilla—is first to notice, and she gives a shriek and jumps back, bumping into John, who was following her lead towards the door.

"What is it?" John says. "Blind people?"

"No, she has a gun!"

"Mom, what's going on?" Anton asks, trying to see.

"Stay behind me," Gina orders him, not taking her eyes off of Camilla.

Nick opens the door to the truck and jumps back inside.

"Jesus," Mark exclaims, his hand going to the back of his belt. "How did you …? Camilla, no!"

He's about to step in front of her, but Camilla sees him coming, and she strides over to Gina.

Gina raises her hands to show them empty, but she doesn't move. If she tries to run, that'll expose Anton, so she has no choice but to stay put.

Everyone is shouting, but Gina tunes it all out. She only sees Camilla coming for her. She hears her labored breath.

Camilla stops in front of her, the gun aimed right at Gina's chin. She's holding it with both hands, and her arms tremble so violently, if she wasn't this close, she might miss the shot. But the barrel is less than three feet from Gina's face, and even a horrible shooter couldn't screw this up.

Gina prepares herself to die, and she only hopes that Anton won't die too. She prays that as soon as Camilla has shot her, Mark or John will jump in and wrestle the gun from her before she can fire again.

But looking into Camilla's wild eyes, Gina realizes it's only her she wants dead. The look of desperation and despair is awfully similar to what she saw in Tommy's eyes right before he left with Fritz.

They sent another poor soul to kill me, Gina realizes. *I wasn't careful enough. I should have thought twice before coming here.*

It feels like the moment has lasted forever, when really, only a blink of an eye has gone by.

"Please don't shoot me," Gina says softly. "I'm afraid you might hurt my son."

It seems like the last word lands on Camilla like a slap. She literally shakes her head briefly, and then a pain so strong it looks almost physically palpable comes forth in her eyes. "If I don't, they'll kill *my* son," she croaks. "They ... they took him ..." She gasps, visibly swallowing the sobs that are pushing to come up through her throat. Her gaze flickers briefly, as though she's seeing someone standing right next to Gina, even though there's no one there. A stray tear rolls from her eye, and she blinks fiercely. "I have to shoot you ... I have no choice ..."

And it all falls into place for Gina. She still hears Mark shouting, feels Anton grip her shirt, but she filters it all out, and she begins talking calmly to Camilla. "I know exactly what you're feeling. I have been in your place. Only a few weeks ago, I killed someone in order to save my son. It wasn't a stranger, either. She was my best friend. And I'll live with the regret forever. All I can do is ask you, for the sake of my son, please don't do this. Please, let me help you get your son back."

Camilla opens her mouth and lets out what is partly a wail, partly the word "no." She sobs and gasps and grinds her teeth. "I can't ... I can't ... they'll kill Danny ... they'll kill him ... I can't ..." Her arms are bobbing and swaying now, so it's very likely that if Camilla squeezes the trigger, the bullet will go astray. Which isn't too much of a comfort for Gina, because it still might hit Anton.

"Please, Camilla," she says, lowering her arms. "I know it's an impossible situation. But if you shoot me, it will never end. Unless we work together, they truly win." She places her hand on her heart. "I swear to you, I will do everything in my power to get your son back."

Camilla obviously hears something, because she flinches, then makes one last effort to bring herself to shoot. She opens her eyes wide, bites down hard, and forces her arms to stay still.

For a breathless moment, it appears she might actually do it.

But Gina can tell she never reaches the tipping point. It comes close. She's really fighting herself. Something—probably the love she feels for her child—wins by a narrow margin, and all of a sudden, all the emotion disappears from Camilla's eyes. Her face goes blank, and with a sigh, she collapses to the ground like a balloon deflating.

Mark jumps in to grab her, but he's too far away.

Gina isn't. She manages to grab Camilla a split-second before her head hits the cobblestone, instead laying it down very gently.

4
CAMILLA

When she wakes up, she feels different. She can tell something has changed inside of her, even before she opens her eyes. Once she does, she finds herself back in Erika's apartment. She's lying on the chaise longue in the living room, a blanket over her legs.

Hoisting herself up onto her elbow, she sees the others seated around the dining table—all of them except Mark.

Gina, her son, the deaf guy, the blind guy, and his daughter. All of them—excluding John—are looking at her quietly.

"How are you feeling?" Gina asks, smiling.

Camilla almost bursts out laughing. It's all coming back to her in big chunks now. She almost shot Gina. Then, nothing. Then cut to Gina asking her warmly how she's feeling.

"I ... I feel all right," Camilla says, realizing to her surprise it's the truth. "Much lighter, somehow ... What happened?"

"You passed out," John says.

Gina gets up and comes over. She sits down by Camilla's feet and places a hand on her shin. "Thanks for trusting me," she says. "You did the right thing."

Those words bring back the final, big part of her memory which was still in darkness until now. She gasps and covers her mouth. "Danny ... Oh, God ..."

"It's all right," Gina says. "We'll get him back. We're discussing our options right now."

Mark comes into the living room. Seeing Camilla is awake, he comes over. She gets up and embraces him.

"I'm so glad you're OK," Mark says, kissing her ear. "Are you feeling all right?"

"I am," Camilla whispers, then begins crying. The tears feel different too. She's not crying out of fear or hopelessness this time, not even out of sadness. It's more like she's crying from ... relief. As though she's letting something go.

Because even though the awful thought of having lost Danny is back, she somehow now experiences it against a backdrop of surprising calm. It's completely counterintuitive. How can anyone in their right mind feel calmness when their baby is missing? Camilla considers briefly the possibility that she's lost her mind. That it's literally broken down under the pressure.

But she can tell that's not the case. The fear is still there, it's just not controlling her. It tries to. Constantly rising up and lashing out, like bursts of melted lava bubbling up from a volcano, reaching for the sky.

But somehow, Camilla is out of reach. Unless she voluntarily jumps down there, the lava can't touch her. And she doesn't feel inclined at all to do that. In fact, she feels not only much safer up here, she can also tell she's much more able to function, which in turn will up her chances of getting Danny back.

This was what Mark tried to tell me, she realizes, holding him out so she can see his face. "Thank you," she tells him.

He smiles a little uncertainly. "For what?"

"I don't know. Just ... thank you. And I love you, Mark."

"I love you too, babe."

She wipes her eyes and turns to the table. "Hello," she says. "Nice to meet you all."

They greet her with nods and smiles.

"Was it ... was it your ghost?" the girl—Lisa—asks. "If you don't mind me asking?"

Camilla nods. "It was. He almost convinced me to do it."

Thinking about how close she came to shooting Gina, she can't help but shiver.

Allan was talking to her from just behind Gina, painting vivid pictures of what would happen to Danny—what might already be happening to him—if Gina didn't die. And Camilla was listening. She couldn't help it. She wanted to shoot Gina. She really did.

Then, just in that moment, when she almost squeezed the trigger, she suddenly, instinctively, shifted her focus away from Gina and into herself. And because Allan was all-out exposing himself, it was easy to feel him inside, too. That wound from so many years ago was not only open, it was bleeding profusely, and it hurt so badly, Camilla almost looked away again.

But she didn't.

She stayed with it. For the sake of Danny. And for young Camilla. The little girl who got abused. Who suffered for all these years. The girl who became the woman who was almost driven to commit murder by her pain.

There was a clear sense of compassion towards her younger self, something she'd never felt before, and there was, even more surprisingly, a tenderness towards Allan as well. In a flash of deep insight, Camilla felt even his pain, which had driven him to do those awful things to her, and she realized how he was merely passing on the hurt, and how he was completely without a choice in the matter, just as she had been up until this moment.

And as she saw it all clearly, she was somehow able to let it all go. And then she chose. She chose not to shoot Gina.

That's when her system finally, mercifully, short-circuited and gave her rest.

Mark pulls out a chair, and Camilla sits down. Gina pours her a cup of coffee, and Camilla takes a sip.

"Okay," she says, looking around at them. "So, how do we do it?"

5
NORA

Her chance comes suddenly, completely unexpectedly, and much sooner than she hoped.

She's filling the tray with mugs and drinking glasses from one of the dishwashers, thinking about nothing in particular, when she suddenly becomes aware of a conversation going on outside the window. It's sitting high up, and it's ajar. A man and a woman are talking in low voices in between drags off of cigarettes.

"I just don't see why she gets to take a nap," the woman says. "I mean, it seems silly."

"I know. Not like she's got a demanding job or anything."

"And did you know she even got her own room?"

"Shut up."

"It's true. That building over there, they put a real bed in it. I saw them bring it in. No worn-out, springy mattress like the rest of us. A real bed." A huff. "She's over there right now, too. Snoring away, while we're slaving away."

"Damn. Wish it was me. Maybe I should ask her if I can sleep next to her."

The woman snorts. "Yeah, good luck with that. As if she'd bed someone like you."

"What's that supposed to mean?"

"Well, you're much older than her. And honestly, I think she's got a little more taste."

The man grunts. "She used to be a drug addict. Her standards can't be that high."

"We're not supposed to talk about anyone's past and you know that. If someone heard—"

"Hey, come on!" another male voice shouts from farther away. "Smoke break was over three minutes ago!"

Nora stands with a mug in each hand, staring up at the window and the broken sky beyond it. Her pulse is thrumming in her ears. She did wonder where the girl had gone, why she hasn't seen her the last couple of days. Generally speaking, there was no sick leave—unless you were in a really bad state—so it was much more likely she'd been reassigned to some other task. Apparently, Nora was right in that theory, and now she also knows where the girl is.

There are other former drug addicts in the Palace. But for some reason, Nora is certain it was the Junkie they were talking about.

She puts down the mugs, wipes her hands in the dish rag, then taps the Stammer on the shoulder.

He jolts and turns around to look at her. "Wh-what?"

"I don't feel too hot. I need to lie down. Could you cover for me? I'm almost done with the mugs."

"S-sure."

"Thanks." He doesn't seem to pick up on the lie in her voice, and Nora turns to the kid. "You, Bomber."

The boy is supposed to sort the cutlery, but he's just standing there, picking up a spoon now and then, looking at it like he's trying to remember what it's for, only to put it back down again. Now, he flinches and looks at Nora. "Yeah?"

"You stay here, okay? Keep doing ... whatever you're doing."

He blinks. "Where are you going?"

"I have to rest. I'm not feeling well."

"Oh. All right."

"Ask the Stammer here if you have any questions."

"Questions?" he repeats dreamily. "About what?"

Nora sighs. "Never mind. I'll see you later."

She leaves them. Going for the bathrooms, she strains not to run. She exits the hangar, but instead of going left towards the showers and toilets, she turns right for the exit. The door is open, held by a wooden wedge, and a group of people enter just as she's about to step out. Judging by the smell coming from them, Nora figures it's the smokers.

Once they've passed, she steps out onto the pavement. She's rarely done so since she arrived here, only feeling the fresh air at dusk or dawn when she goes back and forth between the hangar and the sleeping barracks. Finding herself under the open sky in broad daylight, it's a strange feeling.

Squinting, she looks around. The barracks are right there, stretching towards the landing strips, and a little farther left is another, lonely and much smaller building. Nora never paid much attention to it, because she never had any business going over there, and she didn't even think it was in use. And it probably wasn't. Not until now.

Around the corner of the hangar, where the gate is, she can hear them loading trucks. A forklift is driving around, and big cases filled with weapons are standing in line, waiting to be unpacked.

Nora gets goose bumps for some reason. She doesn't really care what they're doing. It's like it doesn't concern her, and she prefers not to think about it. Fritz hasn't explained it in any kind of detail in the speeches he'll regularly hold, but he has alluded at enemies being out there, growing in numbers and strength, someone who's plotting to derail their cause and kill them all if they get the chance. This is why they need to strike first, and that's exactly what they've been doing. Three times already, they've sent off trucks full of armed men and women. One time, Nora saw them leave, their faces set in stone. Not all of them returned, and those who did were either wounded or look shell-shocked.

People are talking, even though they're not supposed to, and Nora has pieced together that the enemy is the immune people.

Which is kind of strange, because some of the folks here are actually former immune people. Nora has heard quiet talking of that, too. It's not many, probably less than one percent. Whenever she hears anyone mention the immune, she can't help but think of Nick. If he'd been alive, would he have ended up here, just like her? Or would he have had the resolve to stay and fight against these people?

"I miss you, Nick," she whispers, barely aware she's talking out loud.

She remembers vividly seeing his ghost right after he died. The chopping gesture. "Debt." Nora still owes him to set things straight. To get even. To avenge him. She doesn't care about the rules. Plenty of fights are taking place every day. People will suddenly erupt in rage and begin beating someone else senseless. Someone gets killed almost on a daily basis—not to mention suicides. There are at least half a dozen of those a day now.

Some will hang themselves in the barracks, using their belts. Others will use razor blades or broken glass to cut open their jugulars to bleed out in the shower room. Still others will climb the outside fire escape and jump out. Nora has noticed visible, dark stains on the concrete out there.

Whenever someone gets beaten to death, the perpetrator will usually get dragged off, never to be seen again—unless they aren't caught in the act.

More than once, Nora had seen groups of people standing around a bloody, beaten corpse, whenever a fight had gone down without anyone noticing. If there was no one around to blame for it, no one was punished. Which is exactly what she hopes will happen with her and the girl.

She crosses the space between the hangar and the barracks, acting like she's headed over there. She knows all the bunks in the buildings are filled with people snoring away, the early night shifters getting some well-deserved shut-eye.

Reaching the closest barrack, she walks around it, entering the gap between this one and the next. She runs to the other end, stopping briefly by the corner to check if anyone is looking in her direction. She can see the people by the gate of the hangar, but they're all busy. Her heart beating fast, she steps out into the open, then walks to the smaller building.

It hasn't got concrete walls like the barracks, but is built of old, red bricks. Judging from the antenna on the roof, Nora assumes it was some kind of communications office before. She stops by the door to listen. No sounds from inside. So, she opens and slips inside a dim room, closing the door quietly behind her.

Turning around, she finds herself in what used to be an office of some kind. There are large shelves with plastic boxes, and the desks have been pushed to the walls, making room on the floor for a large bed. In it lies a figure, snoring softly. Nora can't see the face, but she can make out her hair.

It's her. It's really her.

Nora is almost dizzy with elation. She can feel the buzz of her pulse all the way out in the tips of her fingers, as she crouches down and slips out the knife.

A strong sense of déjà-vu comes over her. This is the second time she's sneaking up on the girl sleeping, intent on killing her. The first time, Nora had a hammer. Fritz showed up at the last possible second to stop her.

"That's enough," he said, smiling, as he took the hammer from her. "I've seen what I needed to see."

Nora shakes her head, trying to rid herself of the memory.

Focus on Nick. You're doing this for him. The thought is meant to reinforce her resolve. But for some reason, it does the opposite. And it's followed by another, much less certain one: *Would Nick really want this*?

Then her mind conjures up once more the sight of Nick's ghost, signaling the word "Debt." His expression grave. His eyes dark.

Yes, Nora thinks. *Yes, this is what he wanted. This is what I need to do.*

She steps over to the bed, crossing the floor in five long strides. Before she can second-guess herself again, she raises the knife and—

And she sees the baby.

It's wrapped in a blanket, sleeping face-to-face with the girl.

"Jesus," Nora exclaims.

The girl jolts, blinks, and looks up at her. Her eyes turn wide. "No ... please don't."

Nora lowers the knife. "Did you ... did you have a baby?" she asks, realizing it's a stupid question. The girl obviously wasn't pregnant the last time Nora saw her—which was only a couple of days ago. So, she rephrases: "Where did you get it from?"

The Junkie props herself up on her elbow, looking from the knife to Nora's eyes. "If I tell you, will you promise not to kill me?"

Nora feels dizzy. "Yes," she mutters.

The girl checks briefly on the baby, then looks back at Nora and says in a low voice: "The Prophet brought him to me. It's very important that I keep him safe. No one's supposed to know he's here."

Nora frowns. "Whose baby is he?"

The junkie shrugs. "He didn't say. But ..."

"But what?"

The girl looks even more uncomfortable. Then she goes on: "I think he's, like, a hostage. From the way the Prophet spoke about him ... I think he's keeping him here to blackmail someone."

"Jesus," Nora murmurs, feeling the room spinning faster now. Her hands go to her head, and she notices the knife is still in her hand. She drops it to the floor. The sound is loud enough to cause the baby to stir. He grunts and begins whimpering.

The Junkie quickly scoops him up and gets out of bed. She goes to a table with a sink and a microwave. Using one hand, she mixes a bottle of baby formula, then heats it for twenty seconds in the microwave. She looks like she's done it many times before. The baby is gearing up, complaining louder and louder, until the girl plugs the bottle into his mouth. He begins sucking eagerly. The Junkie sits down on the bed again. She looks at the knife Nora had dropped on the floor. Then back up at her face.

"You have come to kill me, right?"

Nora can only gape; no words come out.

"It's OK," the girl sighs. "I knew it would happen sooner or later. I saw it in your eyes. And … I get it." Her lips begin quivering. "I really do. I thought of doing it myself, only I'm too big of a coward. So, really, you'd be doing me a favor." She sniffs and goes on in a weak voice, "I just want you to know my name before you do it."

"No, don't tell me," Nora hears herself say. "I don't want to know anymore."

But the girl tells her anyway. "It's Steffie. My name is Steffie." She shakes her head slowly, her eyes going distant for a moment. "You know how he said it would all go away? The ghosts and everything? I think … I think he lied. I think it's still there. Can't you feel it?"

Nora blinks. "I don't know what you mean."

"Sure you do," the girl goes on. A tear rolls down her cheek, stopping on her jawline, and she uses her shoulder to wipe it away. "I know I'm not seeing him anymore, but ... the stuff he was made of, it's still all inside, it's just ... buried deeper."

Nora swallows. She doesn't want to understand, but she does. Just listening to the girl talk, she can feel it stir deep inside. The pain.

"I feel so fucking guilty," the girl goes on, her voice going even thinner now. She's still talking very low, not wanting to disturb the baby, who's still drinking. "For what I did to your brother. I just want it to go away. That's all I ever wanted. That's what I was doing with the drugs. I see it now, because I'm clean. But this place ..." She looks around with disdain on her face. "It's another kind of drug. We don't need to shoot up, because it's, like, in our souls or whatever. It wasn't until I saw him ..." She looks down at the baby, and a smile comes to her face. "He reminds me so much of my baby brother. I have no idea where he is now. I basically raised him, because my mother was so far gone on heroin. That was back before I started using myself."

This, to Nora, explains how well rehearsed the girl looks in handling the baby.

"I mean, look at him," the girl says, smiling even wider, leaning forward slightly.

And Nora sees the baby's face properly for the first time. He apparently senses her, because he turns his eyes away from the bottle and focuses on her. Nora can tell he can't really see her—the room is too dim, and she recalls something about the eyesight of newborns having a very short range—but it's enough to cause something to burst inside of her. It feels like a dam that was keeping warm water back. Now, with the rocks breaking apart, the water rushes out, splashing all over her insides. Seeing the baby's face, it's like looking at perfect innocence. And in a flash, she sees herself in that face. It's like an out-of-body experience where she's suddenly pulled back through time to see herself as a baby. Then the face shifts to newborn Nick, and then to the girl who's holding the baby. And it keeps going, keeps changing to someone new, all of them just days old, peaceful, joyful, content, unknowing and without a trace of pain or the intention to ever hurt anyone, and as she realizes deeply that this is how they all came into this world, she sees with the utmost clarity how they're all made of the same pure stuff, and that in whichever way they'll later go on to get corrupted, it can never really reach that pureness inside.

Seeing all of this, it's almost too much to hold in her perception, and Nora gasps and takes a staggering step backwards. "Oh, God," she mutters, clasping a hand over her mouth as though to stop the words, but she can't. "This was never what he wanted … How could I … how could I make myself believe Nick would have me …? Oh, Jesus …"

Covering her eyes, her knees give way, and she slumps to the floor. "God … Oh, God … Nick, I'm so sorry … I'm so, so sorry …" The warm stuff is still roaring through her system, and it's painful but also a huge relief, and she has no choice but to allow it all to happen. If it's going to drown her from within, then so be it. "I'm so sorry I wasn't there … Please, forgive me …"

And as she says it, she feels Nick again.

Not as a ghost.

Not as a memory.

But in a very clear, almost violent flash of connection.

She feels the light pressure of a seat against her buttocks. Feels her palms heating up. She smells coffee.

Then it subsides just as quickly as it came.

Nora takes her hands away from her eyes. She stares at Steffie, who's looking back at her, worry on her face.

"Are you ... OK?" she asks.

"Yes," Nora whispers. "I'm fine. And so is Nick." She's not sure if she's about to laugh or cry or both.

Steffie raises her eyebrows. "What, your brother? Are you sure?"

"One hundred percent," Nora says, getting to her feet. "I just felt him. He's with someone else. Drinking coffee. He's alive." She turns and heads for the door.

"Wait!" Steffie calls. "Where are you going?"

Nora looks back. "I'm going to find him, of course."

Steffie shakes her head. "You can't just leave. They'll stop you. They'll kill you."

Nora hesitates. "Damnit, you're right ... But I have no choice. I need to get out of here. I need to find my brother." She never thought she'd ever talk about Nick out loud again, and the words still seem strange in her own ears. But the conviction that Nick is alive and well is still as strong as the feeling of her own heart beating in her chest.

"I have a better idea," Steffie says, putting the bottle aside as the baby is apparently done. "Let me just tuck him in ..."

She gets up, takes the blanket, and ever so gently wraps the baby in it. As she puts him down on the bed, he gives off a satisfied sigh.

"What is it?" Nora demands.

Steffie goes to the wall, reaching up to take down one of the plastic boxes. It seems heavy as she places it on a table and takes off the lid.

Nora leans in to the see what must be a hundred or more smartphones.

"I assume yours is in there somewhere," Steffie says, gesturing to the shelves. "Or in one of the others. So, go fish."

She steps back, and Nora looks at all the phones in front of her.

Then her eyes fall on one in particular. Right there, on top of the pile.

No, that can't be. It's just a similar model.

She picks it up. The cover looks very much like hers. She tries turning it on, but it's dead.

"Do you have a charger?" she asks.

Steffie nods towards the table. There's a power strip. In one of the sockets is a charger. Nora plugs it into the phone. It fits. The screen lights up as she turns it on.

"Fuck, it really is my phone," she mutters. "That's like fate …"

As soon as the phone is ready, she calls up Nick.

She expects it not to work. Expects to get some kind of message about the network being down.

But the call goes through.

She stares at the screen, holding her breath.

6
NICK

Nick is sitting by the table, holding the hot mug with both hands, following the conversation.

"All right," Gina says, smiling at the others. "Now that Camilla is awake, I'll just recap where we stand." She looks at Nick. "We know from what Nick saw that the place is very likely at Airbase Karup. That's in Central Jutland, about two hundred miles from here. I was contacted by Fritz's father, Franz Hagen, who was once on their side, but now is trying to help us, the resistance. Like Fritz, he's able to use doorways as loopholes. He told me it will come to war sooner or later, and we're probably facing several thousand people over there. Whether that's accurate or not, we're definitely outnumbered by a huge margin. The good news is, that doesn't really matter too much. They're more afraid of us than we are of them. It's like a tiny flame burning at night. Even though the darkness is much bigger, it flees from the light wherever the flame goes. We're that flame." She looks down, considering for a moment. "Now, there are two tasks at hand. First, we need to get Danny back, safe and sound. And since we can't count on Franz's help, and we can't open the portals ourselves, it looks like we'll need to make the drive. The second task we've been dealt is to kill the thing that Fritz has fathered." Gina looks at Camilla, and her eyes are very serious now. "This whole thing was brought about by evil entities who want to attain physical existence, so they are born and grow up incredibly fast. It's happening all over the world, but we'll just focus on this one closest to us for now. I'm sure other groups of resistance are forming elsewhere."

"Wait," Camilla says, frowning. "You're saying these things ... they aren't human?"

"Partly, I think," Gina says. "They're like demons in human bodies."

"So, how do we know they can be killed? What if bullets don't work on them?"

Gina licks her lips. "There are two kinds of dangers in this world. Ghosts and predators. So far, we've been dealing with ghosts. And you're right, with those, bullets do nothing. In fact, any kind of aggression usually makes them stronger. That's why love and forgiveness are what rids us of them."

She sends Camilla a significant look at this, and Nick can tell Camilla gets it.

"Predators, on the other hand," Gina goes on, "require different means. You don't scare off a wolf by showing it compassion; you kick it as hard as you can. These ... creatures, they're predators. Bullets will definitely work on them."

"Provided that we don't miss," John adds with a grim face. His broken arm is resting on the table in front of him. "We have no way of knowing what they're capable of."

"That's right, but at least we know what they look like," Gina says, looking at her son. "Anton, will you show it to Camilla?"

The boy pulls out his phone, swipes a few times, then pushes the phone across the table.

Camilla leans forward. Nick already saw the picture, but he can't help but look again.

Anton found it online. It's taken from a phone by someone who was hiding in a bush—evident by the leaves covering some of the view. Right outside some kind of huge building—it looks like a factory—is a group of people all dressed in black. In the middle is a figure that's easily noticeable, because it's close to twice as tall as the others. It's facing the other way, but—almost like it senses the person about to take the photo—it has turned its head just at the right moment, and its face is visible. Even though it's pretty far away, the features are unmistakably nonhuman. Close, but no cigar. To Nick, it feels like looking at something computer-generated. He feels a shiver run down his back.

Camilla seems to feel something similar, because she pushes the phone back to Anton with a grimace. "Jesus ... is that what has taken my baby boy?" Tears form in her eyes.

"We'll get him back," Mark assures her, wrapping an arm around her shoulders.

Gina goes on. "Driving over there might only take a few hours. But I think showing up guns blazing will be a bad idea."

"We could infiltrate them," Mark suggests, still holding Camilla. "We know they're all dressed in black. If there really are that many of them, they probably won't notice a new face. One or two of us could dress up and sneak in there, find Danny and bring him out back, where the rest of you are waiting with the truck."

He looks around the table. The others seem to consider the idea. No one has any objections.

"That's one way we could go about it," Gina agrees. "I have another suggestion. We contact one of the people over there. We know at least three of them. Nick's sister, the girl who took Danny, and of course, Tommy."

This causes the others to shift uncomfortably or exchange strained looks.

"You can't really mean that," Lisa says, not looking up, which makes it hard for Nick to read her lips. "That we reach out to Tommy ... after what he did."

"Nick's sister is of course the obvious choice," Gina goes on, her expression soft. "But if we can't get to her, then I think Tommy should be our second option."

"You honestly think he'll help us?" John asks with a frown.

Gina seems to consider her answer. Then she says: "I don't believe he wanted to do what he did. I believe—"

"Of course he wanted it!" Lisa shouts, looking at Gina with fire in her eyes. "He planned it all out! For days, he was preparing that bomb. How can you say he didn't want it to happen?"

"He was driven by other forces," Gina says calmly. "Just like we've all been at some point. Tommy's actions were just a bit more extreme, but—"

"A bit?" Lisa exclaims, sneering now. "He killed my mom! He killed your son too, Gina! How can you even think of wanting to cooperate with him? He deserves to rot in hell for what he did ..." The girl's face crumbles as she's speaking, and John pulls her into a tight hug with his good arm. She begins sobbing into his chest.

Anton bends his head and begins crying as well. Gina reaches over and takes his hand, squeezing it.

Nick looks down at the table, feeling very uncomfortable. He was always very sensitive to moods, and right now, the atmosphere around the table is dark to say the least.

When he looks up again, Gina begins talking. There are tears in her eyes, too. "I know what Tommy did. But I also know that's only what it looks like on the surface. Really, it wasn't him who killed your mother or my son or all the others we've lost. It wasn't even Fritz. It was the dark forces that we're facing. And they will go on to kill the rest of us if we don't deal with them the right way." She sniffs and shakes her head. "Tommy isn't a ghost, and he's not even a predator. He's a human being, and I know it's very difficult to see right now, but what he deserves …" She swallows, visibly steadying herself. "What he deserves for what he did, is our forgiveness."

Lisa rips free of her dad's arms, gets up and marches out of the room.

Gina stares at John, a single tear rolling from her eye. "I'm very sorry. I don't mean to make anyone upset. I can only speak the truth as I see it."

"I get it," John mumbles. "Give her time."

Gina nods, wiping away the tear, then looking around at them again. "I think Tommy regrets what he did. I think there's a chance we can turn him around. And if we do, he'll be able to get to Danny much easier than any of us can. But, like I said, Nick's sister is our first choice."

They all look at him. He straightens up.

Camilla asks: "Can we call her?"

He takes out his phone and types a quick message: Tried many times.

When Gina has read it out loud, he calls up Nora again. It goes straight to voicemail. He shrugs and puts the phone down on the table.

Gina bites her lip. "If only there was some way of reaching her, without Fritz or anyone else over there knowing about it. Anyone have an idea?"

They exchange looks.

"Let's try Tommy," Mark says, taking out his phone. "I still have his number." He makes the call, but soon shakes his head. "Nothing."

"All right," John says. "We're putting a pin in that one for now. I agree, it's a great opportunity if we can reach one of them. But until then, let's run over our other options. I think if we try …"

Nick stops looking at John's lips, because suddenly, out of nowhere, he feels Nora.

It's hands-down the strongest connection they've ever made. Even stronger than when he felt her just before they passed each other in the cars.

There's so much pain in the connection, it makes him gasp out loud. It's not physical, but deep, emotional pain. It's fear, sorrow, regret, guilt, all mixed into a red-hot ball, and it fills his heart for a second or two, causing his hands to go to his chest.

Then it subsides just as quickly as it came on, leaving him with a clear feeling of Nora.

Nick breathes fast, and he realizes the conversation has ceased. Everyone around the table is looking at him.

"What is it?" Gina asks. "Are you OK, Nick?"

Nick nods. Swallowing, he types on his phone: Just felt my sister. She reached out to me.

Gina reads it out loud. Judging by their faces, not all of them get it.

Gina seems to. "Is it like what happened in the car, right before we split up?"

Nick nods.

"You have some kind of twin connection? Almost like telepathy?"

Nick nods again.

"Is your sister still where Fritz is?"

Again, he nods.

Gina looks around at the others, and there's a moment of quiet contemplation.

Then, Mark asks: "Your sister ... how did she end up there?"

Nick shrugs.

"It doesn't really matter," Mark goes on. "What I'm really asking is, do you think she'll help us?"

Nick nods emphatically. There's not a doubt in his mind that Nora is still on their side. Nothing in this world could ever turn him and her against each other, and no matter what happened to Nora since Fritz brought her to his place, what Nick just felt was much more powerful than that.

"That's great news," Mark says, looking from Nick to the others. "This means we could get an insider. Someone who can open the door for us. If we could just—"

He stops talking, when suddenly, Nick's phone vibrates.

On the screen is Nora's picture.

It's an incoming video call.

7
TOMMY

Why am I still alive?

The question has haunted him ever since he arrived at this place. It keeps popping into his mind. He has no good answer. He honestly doesn't know how he's still breathing. How his body is still functioning. He's barely eating or drinking. His sleep is superficial and full of nightmares. He dreams of explosions. Bombs about to go off. He always tries to diffuse them, but he can't. Unlike the TNT he set off in the safe house, the bombs in his dreams always have old-school fuses, but no matter how much Tommy blows and spits at them, they just keep burning, until finally ... boom. The blast is always strong enough to blow away everything around him. People, cars, buildings. Bodies are torn to shreds, windows are shattered, entire blocks crumble to the ground.

But, surprisingly, Tommy himself is never affected. He's just standing there, feeling the heat and the shock wave knocking against him, but he's somehow rooted to the spot, and there's no pain. Not for him. Only everyone else.

That's when he wakes up screaming. It happens at least six times at night. He'll cry himself back to sleep, knowing all too well as soon as he drifts off, the awful dream will begin again.

Why am I still alive?

Fritz told him all the pain would go away, and he wasn't exactly lying. Tommy can feel the dreams getting less intense. The memories are starting to fade, details that were burned into his mind are suddenly missing.

But it'll take time. It's a lot to swallow. He tried to ask the Twin for help, but she just told him to be patient.

"How did you end up here?" he asked her, even though he knew they weren't allowed to speak of it. But it was the middle of the night, and everyone else in the barrack was sleeping soundly.

She sighed and told him she came to this place because she tried to kill someone.

"So you didn't actually go through with it?"

"I would have," she told him in a serious tone. "If Fritz hadn't stopped me at the last moment."

Tommy felt envious. Why couldn't Fritz have stopped him too? He could have come in after Tommy had placed the bomb, taken the controller from him, and done the rest himself.

Of course, Tommy would probably still feel guilty. He would still be the murderer. The reason all those people are dead.

I should be dead, just like them.

Victor and Patrick he knows for sure are gone. Patrick was still trying to diffuse the bomb when it went off. And Victor he saw with his own eyes, lying in Gina's arms. That image is—thankfully—also starting to go hazy.

Tommy didn't look too closely at the monitor after the bomb went off—everything was smoke and dust anyway—so he doesn't know for sure who else is dead. Perhaps Gina is the only one who made it. Perhaps Otto, Lisa, John, even Rex ... perhaps they're all blown to pieces.

As he was suffocating in the basement and rushing upstairs, Tommy had taken the claustrophobia to be just that. Now, he understands it was really the truth that came rushing at him. Because the moment it happened, the second that bomb went off, that was when Tommy's dad disappeared, and with him went the haze Tommy had been living in. The spell he was under, it was blown away just like the safe house, and he could suddenly see what he'd done—what his ghost had convinced him was the only right thing to do.

And it was too much.

Tommy feels certain that if he'd had to take it all in, to realize fully what he'd done, it would have suffocated him for real. His chest would have imploded under the terrible weight of all those lives on his consciousness, crushed his lungs in an instant, stopped his heart from beating.

Perhaps that's the right to do. To simply let the truth come and kill him. Let karma squash him like a bug. It's what he deserves.

Tommy misses his dad. Misses him dearly. Having him by his side, he at least had someone to talk to. Now, he's all alone, even though he's surrounded by people.

He knows his dad was just a ghost, and he's even aware that he was the one who drove Tommy to do what he did.

Still, there's no anger. Only sorrow and loss.

On an intellectual level, Tommy understands he was deceived by an evil entity masquerading as his deceased father.

On an emotional level, he's a lost child, alone and scared, desperately longing for his daddy.

On the outside, Tommy is a ruthless killer—the Bomber, they call him, and people send him acknowledging nods and smiles, impressed with what he did to their dreaded adversaries.

On the inside, Tommy is a shaky leaf, blowing hither and dither, wanting only to find safety and peace in a world where everything hurts.

Why am I even here? Tommy thinks, looking at the fork he's holding for some reason. *If I'm just waiting to die, then I might as well get it over with.*

It would be easy. He could plunge the fork into his eye.

The idea comes out of nowhere. It's both terrifying and oddly inviting. If he did it properly, he might not even feel any pain.

The thought of seeing his father again almost makes him cry with relief. Of course, if Kent Jansen is there, so are all the others. The people he killed. And Tommy will have to face them.

Something else is holding him back too. Perhaps it's fear, perhaps he's simply a coward. Or maybe it's because Tommy is scared that what he'll meet in the afterlife won't be the soul of his real father, but the ghastly figure he's already familiar with, the grim imitation bound to the hospital bed. The thought of spending eternity with that entity isn't exactly enticing.

Or maybe it's something else entirely. Somehow, it just feels like it wouldn't be right. Not yet, at least.

There's still something I need to do.

He can't explain where the feeling is coming from, but it rings true. There's one last task for him in his life. One more purpose he needs to fulfill. He just doesn't know what it is yet.

His bladder reminds him it needs to be emptied. He turns to the Stammer and says: "I have to take a bathroom break."

"S-sure," the guy answers, barely looking at him.

Tommy weaves his way to the exit.

He finds all four stalls occupied. The last one isn't technically taken by anyone, but a dead woman is lying on the floor, both her wrists cut open, a knife lying next to her in a pool of blood. Looking at her, Tommy feels surprisingly indifferent.

He goes outside, steps away from the door and unzips his pants. As he starts peeing on the wall of the hangar, something catches his eye. Turning his head, he sees a woman—it looks like the Twin—run from the barracks to another, much smaller building.

She stops by the door, glances back quickly—guiltily—and then slips inside.

Tommy has stopped peeing, and he zips his pants back up. He looks around to see if anyone else is around. No one is. He was the only one who saw the woman enter the building.

What's in there?

Tommy has no idea. But he's curious. The way the woman moved, it was obvious she didn't want to be noticed.

Tommy is about to go there, when a group of people comes out the door. They all begin lighting up cigarettes.

One of them—a young guy with a scruffy beard—notices Tommy standing there. "'Ey, you need a smoke?"

"Thanks," Tommy mutters, taking the pack without really thinking. "I was all out."

"Glad I could help," the guy says, handing Tommy a lighter.

They all stand there, smoking in silence for a moment. Two of the women speak about nothing in particular.

Then the bearded guy turns his head to look at Tommy. "You're the Bomber, right?"

Tommy swallows. "I am."

"'Ey, man. Nice job. You're a hero."

Tommy inhales deeply, filling his lungs with smoke. "Yeah, I know."

"I mean, I heard you blew up a couple of kids, too. That's gotta be rough to live with, I get that. But 'ey, better them than us, right? They would have come for us if you hadn't stopped them."

Tommy can't look at the guy. He feels like puking and crying at the same time. He just keeps smoking.

The guy drops his butt and steps on it. Exhaling the last lungful of smoke, he leans closer to Tommy and whispers: "We've all got shit we're trying to forget. Just let it go, man. Get on with your life. You deserve it."

Then he goes back inside along with the other.

Tommy waits until he's alone. Then he runs to the lone building. Stopping by the door, he listens.

He can hear two females talking inside. One of them is definitely the Twin. The other, Tommy can't remember having heard before. Leaning closer, he picks up on what they're saying. At first, he has no idea what the conversation is about.

But he keeps listening.

8

GINA

Gina sees a picture of a young woman on Nick's phone. She looks very much like him, only with long hair. She doesn't need to read the name to know it's his twin.

"It's her," Anton gasps, looking from the phone and up at Nick. "Pick it up! What are you waiting for?"

Nick doesn't catch it, because he's staring at the phone.

Gina reaches over and nudges his shoulder.

He blinks, glances at her briefly, then answers the call.

The picture of Nora disappears and is replaced by a live image of her, seen from an angle slightly below her face. She's obviously holding the phone in her hands, because the image is shaking a bit. She's somewhere where the lights are turned down, and her face is full of hope and trepidation.

"*God, Nick,*" she says, a hand coming into view to cover her mouth for a second. Then, letting her brother see what she's saying, she removes the hand again. "*I can't believe it … You're really OK!*"

Nick lets out a noise somewhere between a sob and sigh. Gina hasn't been around him for that long, but she's already noticed how seldomly he makes any kind of sound. He's obviously moved, fighting to hold back the tears. He props the phone against his mug and makes a series of rapid movements with his hands.

"Yes, I'm fine," Nora says, smiling through tears. "*Better than ever, now that I know you're alive.*"

Nick smiles and replies something.

"*I know, I have tons of things to tell you, too. Where are you? Are you safe?*"

Nick nods, saying something with his hands.

"Oh," his sister says. "*Who are they?*"

Nick hooks his index fingers together, then makes another sign which looks like he dusts something from off the back of his hand. Then he picks up the phone and pans it around, showing them all the screen one at a time. They all nod or mutter "hi."

"Hi, everyone," Nora says. "*I'm Nora, Nick's sister. He tells me you're all his friends, and most of you are immune.*"

Nick hands the phone to Gina. "Hi, Nora," she says with a smile. "I'm Gina. I think I speak for all of us when I say we're very glad to meet you. Can I ask, where are you right now?"

Nora looks briefly around the dim room, then back at the screen. "*I'm still at the Palace, but I'm in a safe place. There's one other person here with me. Well, two, actually ...*" She flips the phone around, showing a young woman sitting on a bed.

Gina recognizes her right away. She looks just as gaunt and worn as the last time they met. "Hello, Steffie," she says.

Out of the corner of her eye, she notices Nick stiffen up as he reads the word off her lips. He stretches his neck, trying to see the screen, but Nora has already turned the camera back on herself. As she sees Nick leaning into frame, her expression turns to something between remorse and uneasiness. "*Nick, I know how it looks, but I can explain ...*"

Nick frowns and signals something which Gina catches: He mimics shaving himself with a finger, then taps the Band-Aid still sitting on his neck.

"*I know what she did,*" Nora says, sounding rueful. "*Look, it's hard to tell you this over the phone, but you need to trust me. She did a terrible thing, and she did it because she felt she had to. That she had no real choice. I get it, because that's exactly what I did. I found her, Nick.*" Nora's voice becomes thinner. "*After I thought I'd lost you, I found Steffie, and I ... I was going to bash her brains in. I would have done it, if that guy, Fritz, he hadn't showed up at the last moment ...*"

Nora mentioning Fritz's name causes everyone—especially Mark and Camilla—to sit up a little straighter.

"*He made the pain go away,*" Nora whispers. Her eyes are gleaming with tears. "*At least that's what he promised would happen. But ever since I came here, I've been obsessed with killing Steffie, paying the debt I owed to you, Nick, for not being there when you needed me. I couldn't save you like you saved me from the jellyfish. And I almost went through with it again, just ten minutes ago ...*" Nora is crying now, but she keeps talking. "*But then I forgave her, Nick. And I forgave myself. I hope you can, too. But if not, then I understand. I don't want to carry around this awful burden anymore. It's making me do awful things. It's turning my love for you into something horrific, and it's not real ...*" She shakes her head, and suddenly, she smiles through the tears. "*It's not real, Nick. None of it. The hate, the fear ... it's just ... I don't know, a mirage. I hope you understand, because I don't know how else to explain it ...*"

"We understand," Gina says. "You've gone through what several of us have, too."

Nora wipes her nose. "*I'm very relieved to hear that. I thought I might have lost it.*"

"I considered that too when it happened to me," Gina tells her with a reassuring smile. "But I think it's quite the opposite."

Nora nods, then looks at her brother. "*Nick? Please tell me what you're thinking.*"

Gina glances sideways. Nick is just sitting there, staring at the phone, his expression blank. He seems to be pondering a deep question, and he's apparently unaware that his fingers are fiddling with the edges of the Band-Aid. Then he inhales deeply and holds his hand palm up. With the other, he strokes it twice, as though dusting it off.

Nora sighs out loud. Squeezing her eyes shut, she places one hand on her heart and whispers: "*I love you, Nick.*"

Nick sniffs, blinks away a tear, then shows Nora what to Gina looks like a devil sign: a fist with his thumb, pinky and index finger raised. He gets up from the table and walks to the other end of the living room. He doesn't seem to have any objective, other than needing a little space, so Gina clears her throat and goes on: "Nick's still here, he's just taking a breath. You said there was someone else there with you too?"

Nora nods, clearing her throat. "*Yes, and I have no idea who he is, but I have a feeling you guys might. Here, let me show you ...*"

Nora goes to the bed, turns the phone over, and holds it close to the face of a baby boy sleeping soundly, wrapped in a blanket.

Gina's heart leaps.

"Oh, my God," Anton exclaims. He's standing behind Gina, looking over her shoulder. "Is that … is that him?"

"What is it?" Mark asks, his brows furrowed, his eyes darting back and forth between Gina and Anton. "What are you seeing?"

Camilla doesn't wait for them to answer. She gets up, almost knocking over her chair in the process, and runs around the table. Staring at the screen, she lets out half a scream, half a gasp. "Danny!"

9
TOMMY

Tommy listens for a long time.

Once the phone call finally ends, he runs back to the hangar.

He's heard everything he needs to.

Instead of going back to the kitchen area, Tommy heads for the bathrooms. The last stall, the one where the dead lady was lying, is now empty. Most of the blood has been mopped up.

Tommy closes the door and sits down on the lid. He begins bopping his knees up and down, staring at a bloodstain on the door that whoever cleaned up the stall must have missed. It looks like a rifle pointing at the sky.

Yes, Tommy thinks, his head feeling oddly empty. *That's what I need.*

He feels anxious, almost to the point of nausea, but at the same time, there's also a feeling of resignation. Of acceptance.

Ever since the crack in the sky first appeared, Tommy's life has been one long spiral of disasters. He's lost everything and everyone, and his actions have become more and more out of control and violent.

He tries to think back, even though his memory is still kind of hazy, tries to pinpoint the moment in time when he crossed the line—what was it they called it in school? The point of no return.

Was it when he saw his mother die?

Was it when he opened the door for Melissa back at the safe house?

Maybe when he stabbed Johan to death?

Or that tiny moment in which he decided to not tell Otto that his dead father was still around?

The biggest turning point was no doubt the bomb. But Tommy suspects it happened before that. Could it have been way earlier? Perhaps even before the sky started breaking? Back when he lost his dad, maybe. Or earlier still. His childhood, with an absent-minded mother and an abusive father.

Tommy can't tell. It's difficult thinking back. It's like his mind doesn't want to go there.

Imagining his life as a character in a novel, it would definitely be in the horror genre. Probably written by Stephen King or someone just as gruesome and disregarding of the characters he'd created. Only a madman would think up a relatively normal and healthy teenage boy, only to have him go through hell with no hope of redemption.

Except …

That wasn't true.

There had been hope. Every step of the way, he had had a choice. Right up until the final moment. The second before he stepped through that doorway with Fritz. Even he had admitted it: "It's your choice, Tommy."

And he had chosen as he always did: the easier of the options. He had made the decision that brought him a small, immediate relief, a respite from the pain and fear. But it also brought him one step farther down the staircase he had been descending for months, if not years.

And now, it was really too late.

Or was it?

"I forgive you, Tommy."

Hearing Gina's voice in his mind, he almost bursts into tears. Covering his mouth with both hands, he manages to hold back the sobs. Instead, his entire body begins trembling violently.

"None of this is ultimately your fault."

But of course, it is.

He plunged the knife into Johan. *He* lied to them all. *He* set off the bomb.

No one else.

"Don't listen to that nonsense," Fritz had told him. *"There's nothing here for you but pain and misery."*

And that was definitely true.

Fritz had promised him he could keep on living. Having killed all those people didn't need to be the end. He could even find a new purpose.

But then again ... wasn't that also what Gina had told him? She wanted him to stay. She wanted him to face it all and then—

"Forgive him. Forgive yourself."

He can't do that. He just can't. What he's done, it is too big to forgive.

And forgiving his father isn't necessary, because Tommy doesn't have any anger towards him any longer. No resentment. Which, come to think of it, is kind of curious, seeing as how the ghost of his father had been there all along, nudging him to go through with the awful things.

"It wasn't really him," Tommy whispers to the empty stall. "My real dad died years ago. Lucky bastard. Got to leave all the shit behind ... including me." Those last two words slip out on their own accord, and almost as an afterthought, Tommy adds: "He left me."

To his surprise, he actually does feel a surge of anger. Though it's very faint. More like a passing annoyance. But it's definitely there. It feels like something is dampening the emotion. As though he's been drugged.

It's this place, he realizes, blinking absently. *That's what Fritz meant. It slowly buries everything.*

"It'll all go away forever."

That's how he put it.

Out of sight, out of mind. That's been Tommy's motto for as long as he can remember. He never cared to dwell on his problems. Just ignore and move forward.

It had worked so far.

But this. This was too big to move on from.

"Your father loved you more than anything."

Another stab in his heart, and this time, he can't help but cry. Bending his head, wrapping his arms around himself, Tommy sobs like a little kid.

As he's crying, faint memories fly through his mind. Tommy, six years old. First school day. His dad was there, smiling at him whenever Tommy got nervous. Tommy, eight years old. Playing soccer in the backyard. His dad let him score the winning goal, even though he could have easily stopped the ball. Tommy, fourteen years old. His dad coming to his room to relay the bad news. Tommy didn't start crying when he heard the word "cancer." Still, his dad hugged him tightly.

"I can't forgive him," Tommy croaks, as the crying finally subsides. "I can't let him go."

"*Stay, Tommy,*" Gina whispers in his mind. "*Believe it.*"

"No," Tommy hisses. "I can't. Without him, I have no one."

He swallows hard, wipes his face in his shirt, and then his gaze falls on the blood stain again.

And suddenly, he gets it.

What Fritz was talking about. He sees it with surprising clarity.

What he needs to do.

What his purpose is.

Tommy inhales deeply. For the first time in a long, long while, he's able to breathe all the way in. As he exhales, almost all of the tension leaves him.

He feels calm. Clearheaded.

He still has a choice.

And he just chose.

10

JOHN

His arm hurts.

The painkillers Camilla found for him in the kitchen cupboard are taking the edge off, but only enough that John still feels clearheaded. He wants to be able to think, or he'll be of no use to anyone. Being blind, his best contribution to the group is not his physical strength, but his knowledge and analytical mind.

So, he ignores the throbbing waves radiating from his elbow and instead focuses on listening to whoever is talking. They've been at it for quite a while now—John no longer has the luxury of looking at a clock, so time feels different—but he's pretty sure it's getting close to sunset. They've gone through more than four pots of coffee. Anton is sleeping in the bedroom, and on the chaise lounge is Lisa, who returned after ten minutes or so, mumbled an apology to Gina, hugged her, and then went to lie down. John can hear her breathing softly in her sleep.

Around the table are Mark and Camilla, John, Gina, and Nick. On the phone is Nora, who acts as interpreter for what Nick is saying with his hands. The dog seems to be curled up next to Lisa, because John hears it sigh now and then.

Poor guy. He lost his entire family.

Rex might have taken the heaviest loss, but they all lost someone. Nick is separated from his sister, who might not make it out of there alive. Mark and Camilla have lost their baby boy. Lisa's mom died just hours ago, and Gina and Anton lost their son and brother.

John is surprisingly affected by his own loss, too. Karen's death still seems kind of unreal to him. He wasn't aware of how much love he still carried for his ex-wife. Apparently, having lived together for years, made love thousands of times, and raised a child together, all that couldn't be erased by a few years of being separated.

Still, John needs to function, so he firmly sets aside the grief for later, and he gets the feeling the others are doing the same. They're all tense, all worried about what's to come. The anxiety is ripe in the air.

But there's also an atmosphere of optimism.

It's different from anything John has felt so far. Somehow, them being together, talking over their options, planning how to proceed, it seems to produce some kind of ... hope is too strong a word, but at least a feeling of opportunity. An unspoken expectation that there's actually something they can do. That despite how dire the situation looks, they are now in a position of taking a stab at setting it right. Some of it, at least.

They might not succeed. In fact, the detective in him, the rational, fact-adhering, probability calculating part of his brain, it tells him the odds are pretty damn awful. Facing a nonhuman creature, a demon born into flesh and bone, possessing God only knows what kind of abilities, he doesn't think it likely many—if any—of them will walk away from that.

Still.

At least they are going to try.

Which gives him a chance. Tiny as it may be, a chance is still a chance.

"All right," Gina says. "Let's sum it up. First, Nora goes back and pretends like nothing happened. At midnight, she'll pick up Danny and meet us at the south-east end of the airfield, by the trees. She'll prepare the message for Fritz and make sure to place it somewhere he'll find it. Then we all leave the same way we came, and we drive straight for the location. Mark, you'll guide us to Erika's parents' beach cabin, which is where we'll make our stand."

A long moment of silence.

John clears his throat. "And, uhm, what Nick saw this guy do ... making people turn their own weapons against them ... that means guns are out, right?"

"I think at least we need to be very careful," Gina says. "Back at the house, when I confronted Fritz, I believe he tried to use this trick on me, but it didn't work. I don't know why or how, but I don't think he can take control over me. Perhaps it's true for all of us who've dealt with our ghosts, but we probably shouldn't assume so. If we all show up with guns, and Fritz really is able to control our movements ... well, it'll all be over quickly."

"So, you're the only one who'll be armed?" Camilla asks Gina.

"I think that's the wisest course, yes," Gina says. "The less weapons, the better. I'll keep mine out of sight, just to be on the safe side."

"*And that's also the reason why we can't do what that kid—Tommy—did, right?*" Nora asks over the phone. "*Just place a bomb right next to the door and blow Fritz to pieces the moment he steps through.*"

"That's right," Gina says. "Since Fritz can make objects move, I'm sure he'll defuse it right away. Or, worse, he might use it on us."

"What if Fritz doesn't come alone?" John asks. "He could get a bunch of people with weapons to follow him."

"If anyone other than Fritz tries to come through, Mark will shut the door," Gina says. "Which he'll do anyway the moment Fritz is through."

"And what about the creature?" Camilla asks. "What if Fritz brings it along?"

Gina doesn't reply right away. The others wait for her answer. In the silence, John can hear Gina breathe evenly as she considers it.

"Then we'll kill it," she says finally. "We will have to do it sooner or later anyway, and I think sooner is better, because from what Franz told me, they grow very big and very strong very fast."

"And you're absolutely sure this thing can be put down with bullets?" John asks. "Because if it shows up and it's unkillable, then we're all just sitting ducks."

"I can't give any guarantees," Gina concedes. "I can only go on what Franz said. All I can say is that everything else he told me seems to hold true, and I find no reason for him to have lied about this."

Another pause in the conversation.

Then, Mark speaks. "I think there's one thing we're overlooking. The door. If I pull it off the hinges, that won't really prevent Fritz from going back, will it? And others can still follow him, because the portal will still be open, right?"

"That's right," Gina says. "The portals only close when the doors close. Good catch, Mark. I guess you need to slam the door, then open it again, *before* lifting it off the hinges. That should cut the portal."

"I don't like Mark being that close to Fritz," Camilla interjects. "I mean, for him to close the door, he'll have to be standing right behind it. Fritz will no doubt hear him."

"You're right," John says. "We can't expose Mark like that. I have a better idea." He senses the others looking at him. He turns his face in the direction of Mark. "You say this cabin, it's made of wood?"

"Yes. It's one of those movable things. Very small and lightweight."

"Then let's set it on fire," John says with a shrug of his good arm. "We'll douse the whole thing in gas beforehand, then strike a match the moment Fritz comes through. That should make him unable to go back, plus, it'll deter anyone else from coming through."

"I like that idea," Mark says. "A cozy fire on the beach. We could even bring marshmallows."

The joke produces a few grunts, and the mood is lifted slightly.

"So, besides the gasoline, we'll also bring medical supplies," John goes on. "Bandages, tourniquets, gauze, antiseptic solution, even tweezers and a sewing kit to remove bullets. Basically everything we could possibly need in case any of us gets hurt."

"You are one thorough guy, Agent Nygaard," Mark says.

John shrugs. "I like to be prepared, that's all. I know where we can find everything; it'll just be a short stop on the way."

"Good," Gina says. "All right, I think we've covered everything. Nora, are you clear on how you'll get Danny to the meeting place?"

"*Yes*," Nora says. "*Steffie just agreed to help me.*"

"Will you come along, Steffie? We'll be happy to bring you." When no answer comes, Gina adds: "You don't need to go with us to the beach; we can drop you off wherever you like."

"*She says no*," Nora tells them. "*She doesn't want to leave.*"

"Fair enough," Gina says. "Thank you for your help, Steffie. If you change your mind, it's a standing offer. Nora, we'll text you when we're ten minutes out. Until then, please be careful, and keep Danny safe."

"*No need to worry*," Nora says. "*We'll make sure he—oh, he's awake.*" John can hear a baby whimpering in the background. Then Nora asks: "*You guys, uhm ... you want to tell him hello?*"

Camilla lets out a gasp, then whispers: "Yes, please. If you could hold the phone close to him. I want him to hear my voice ..."

John doesn't want to listen in on the very personal conversation, so he gets up and moves carefully around the table. He can hear Gina and Nick getting up too. Finding the chaise lounge, he feels for Lisa and finds her legs. As he squeezes her ankle, she grunts.

"Sorry to wake you, sweetheart. But we need to pack up. We're leaving."

"Oh. Okay." Lisa yawns and sits up. "I had the best dream. I was back before this whole thing started. Everything was OK. You and Mom were still ..." Her voice falters.

John reaches out and pulls her into a one-armed hug. "It'll all be OK again. I promise you. We just have this one thing left to do."

Lisa doesn't answer. He can tell she doesn't really believe him.

"What is it, sweetie?"

"It's just ..." She lowers her voice. "Even if we manage to kill this thing, what about all the others? If there are hundreds or even thousands all over the world, what good does killing one do?"

John considers his answer. "Don't think of it that way. That's like preparing for a marathon by telling yourself that one little step doesn't make a difference, so why even bother? Who knows what will happen when we take this first step, huh? What if killing one turns out to be the hard part, and the others will prove much easier? My point is, we have no choice, so we might as well keep hope."

Lisa mutters something.

"What's that?"

"I said, it'll be blind hope."

John smiles. "That's the only kind I'm capable of these days."

Lisa grunts. "All right, Dad. I'll stay optimistic."

"That's my girl," John says, kissing the top of her head. "Now, please get dressed."

11
TOMMY

Tommy needs a weapon.

No explosives this time. It has to be a firearm. Not a handgun, either. A bigger one. A much more deadly one.

He already noticed the trucks out front, and the military boxes piled up under the overhang. He's watched enough war movies to know what's in them, so he heads outside and walks around the building.

Gina and the others are coming. He knows the place. The Twin—Nora—told them to come in from the south, since there's a row of pines over there, running along the side of the airstrip.

It will go down around midnight. Which is clever. The dark will give them cover. Most of the people around here will be sleeping, save for the night shifters. They agreed to text Nora ten minutes before they arrive. Then, she will go to the building where the baby is kept, and she'll bring it along.

The other woman, the Junkie, she wouldn't come. They offered to bring her along, but she declined. Said there was nothing for her out there. Instead, she will pretend that Nora has knocked her unconscious in order to steal the baby. That way, Fritz hopefully won't have her killed. Tommy isn't too sure about that. He's seen the shriveled-up corpse hanging from the ceiling of the hangar, nailed to a big, wooden cross. When he asked the Stammer about it, he said the poor guy had let Fritz down somehow.

That's none of my business, Tommy reminds himself as he strides along the outside of the hangar. *I need to focus on my task.*

It's kind of nice, feeling like his old self again. Not his old-old self, but the more recent version, the one he was just before he arrived here. The confident Tommy. The Tommy who had things to do. The Tommy who would have conversations with his dead father. That seems to be the only difference between then and now: The ghost of his dad doesn't show up, and it doesn't speak inside his mind, either. Tommy keeps expecting to hear its voice, but so far, it's only his own, dark thoughts in there.

Need to get a proper gun. One that'll spray a lot of bullets in a short amount of time.

He reaches the overhang. Half a dozen men are loading boxes into a plane.

The closest one—a short, fat guy who's sweating buckets—turns and sneers at Tommy. "Piss off, kid."

Tommy doesn't move. The men keep loading.

As the fat guy picks up another box, he notices Tommy is still standing there. "Hey, didn't you hear me, boy? Fritz said no looky-loos. So get lost, or I'm gonna kick your—"

"Shut your fucking mouth, Snowman!" One of the others—an older guy with a receding hairline and thin-rimmed glasses—sends the fat guy a significant stare. "You don't know who that is?"

The Snowman—probably named after his round physique—glares Tommy up and down. "He's a fucking nosy-pants, that's who he is."

"I'm the Bomber," Tommy hears himself say. His voice is strained, due to his jaw being clenched. "And you don't fucking talk to me that way."

All the men have stopped working now to look at Tommy. He doesn't give a damn.

The fat guy's eyes grow comically big and round, to the point where they look like they might pop from his meaty face. "Oh ... I'm ... shit ... My apologies, Bomber ... I didn't ... I didn't recognize you just there ..."

"No," Tommy says. "You didn't. And you probably don't know what I did to get here either. Do you?"

The Snowman nods vigorously, causing his double-chin to flap. "I sure do, Bomber. You bombed an entire group of resistors. Killed 'em all before they could come here and hurt us."

"That's right," Tommy says. "And now I've got another assignment." He pries his eyes off the Snowman, looking instead up at the old guy, who's standing on the ramp to the plane. "You, I need a weapon. The Prophet said I could get one here."

"Sure, sure," the skinny guy says, nodding his bald head. His long neck and crooked nose make him look like a big bird. "We're just loading these for the raid tomorrow. Fritz found another group, you heard that? Hiding in a church, of all places. Huh. Should be easy to get to them, right?" The guy laughs nervously, and the screechy sound makes him seem even more like a bird. He clears his throat. "Anyway, whaddya looking for, Bomber?"

"Something that'll do a lot of damage in a very short time," Tommy says. "And it needs to be easy to use."

"Give him one of the automatics, Vulture," another guy chimes in, nodding towards a stack of boxes inside the plane. "I just strapped them down."

The old guy—fittingly named the Vulture—immediately goes to work unstrapping the boxes. He opens the lid of the top one, and takes out the biggest firearm Tommy ever saw in his life. He's only ever seen anything like it in pictures of American troops in the Middle East.

"This good?" the old guy asks, showing it to Tommy.

He pretends to consider it. "Is that the fastest-firing one we got?"

"I—I don't know …"

"It is," the other guy says—the one that suggested this weapon to Tommy. He's younger, dark-skinned and talks with a slight accent. "Fires close to a thousand rounds per minute. Should take down whoever you're shooting at before they can blink."

"That'll do," Tommy says, reaching up his hands.

The Vulture places the weapon back in the box, then carefully hands it over. Tommy begins to feel a bit nervous. The men are still staring at him, and he's afraid one of them will ask about his assignment. He doesn't want to tell them, and he doesn't want Fritz to know. This is his job; no one else's.

He turns to leave, when the Arabic guy calls: "Hey, Bomber?"

Tommy whips around to glare at him. "What?"

"You need ammo, don't you?"

"Oh. Right."

The guy brings him a big metal case with a leather strap on top. "Here you go. Four belts. Should be plenty."

"Thanks," Tommy says.

"Look, uhm," the fat guy says as Tommy is about to leave. "You wouldn't, uhm, tell the Prophet about that little, uhm ... misunderstanding ... would you?"

Tommy stares at him, letting him squirm for a moment. "No," he says.

The Snowman lets out a long sigh, then smiles. "Thank you, Bomber. That's a big relief."

The skinny guy laughs in that scratchy, high-pitched fashion. "You're such a moron, Snowman. Hey, Bomber, you know why Fritz dubbed him Snowman? It's not just because he's shaped like one, you know. It's also because he's melting."

The other men guffaw at this. Tommy can't help but smile.

The Snowman whips his head around, causing droplets of sweat to go flying. "Oh, yeah?" he grunts. "Well, you know why they named that asshole Vulture, then? It's not just because he looks like a stupid bird ..." The Snowman looks at Tommy, his eyebrows raised. "It's because he fucking ate dead people ..."

"Hey!" the skinny guy croaks, pointing a shaky finger at the Snowman. "I told you that in confidence ..."

"Yeah, well, fuck your confidence! You're constantly on my case because I'm not a walking skeleton like you ..."

As the men begin shouting at each other, Tommy slips away.

He's so busy getting out of sight, that as he steps behind a parked truck, he almost trips over a girl sitting on the ground.

"Ouch!" she cries out, slapping his leg with a stick. "Watch out, idiot!"

Tommy is too surprised to react at first. The girl is young, probably the youngest person Tommy has seen around here so far. Her hair is red and shining in the sunlight. He's pretty sure he knows her name; he heard someone whisper about her.

She's the girl who took the baby. The girl Gina mentioned.

"Alicia?" he blurts out.

12
FRITZ

"Dad? Daddy?"

Someone's nudging him.

Fritz grunts and rolls onto his side. He doesn't want to wake up. He's having a pleasant dream. It's about Melissa. She's alive, and all is well. They're on a beach somewhere tropical, sharing chocolate cake and champagne while enjoying the sunset. They're celebrating some kind of anniversary.

Part of him knows it's a dream. Still, he doesn't want it to end just yet.

"Daddy?"

Someone shakes him. The dream dissipates. The sunny beach is replaced by the dim, blood-stinking office. The light, joyful feeling of being with Melissa turns into aches and heaviness all over his body.

Frej is sitting on the edge of the bed, his face hovering above Fritz, his eyes big and serious. "Are you awake, Dad?" His voice is noticeably deeper than just last night.

"Yeah," Fritz murmurs, swinging his legs to the floor. He feels older, too, but not in a good way. Unlike his son, Fritz isn't growing bigger and stronger; he's aging rapidly. These past weeks have been incredibly hard on his body, and as his job draws to a close, he feels the energy that's been fueling him gradually simmer down, leaving him worn and exhausted. He actually looks forward to passing on the mantle to Frej. To retire and enjoy his declining years, knowing that he helped pave the way for the new and better world. "What is it, son?" he asks, grabbing the water bottle from the nightstand. "Are you hungry?"

To his surprise, Frej shakes his head—he's getting better at these small gestures. "Something's wrong."

Fritz hesitates with the bottle resting against his lips "What? Something happened?"

"I'm not sure. But Gina isn't dead yet."

It's not only Frej's body and mind that are evolving with impressive speed. He's also starting to talk of things he should have no way of knowing about. Like what's going on in the world, how the other gatherings are doing, how he feels the pull from his brothers and sisters, and how he can sense Gina as the big, poisonous fly in their ointment. Apparently, Frej has inherited the abilities of the voices. It only makes sense, of course; he might have needed the genetic blueprint from Fritz, along with the womb of Melissa, but he's clearly also descendent from something else. He's the living embodiment of the blind gods. The mighty entities born into flesh, finally able to see the world. To move in it. To shape it to their liking.

Fritz takes a swig of water. "We need to be patient, son. I'm sure Hoffman will—"

"I can't feel Hoffman any longer."

Fritz lowers the bottle. "That's not good."

Frej nods with emphasis. "Exactly. It can really only mean one thing …"

"Now, now, let's not jump to any conclusions," Fritz says, putting the bottle back. "There are other possible explanations. When did you lose him, exactly?"

"Sometime during the night. I don't know. I just woke up, and I couldn't feel him anymore."

Fritz frowns. "You don't think they …?"

Frej's expression is dark. "It's the only thing that makes sense. He's either dead, or in Gina's company. Whichever it is, it's bad news."

Fritz suddenly feels a surge of fury. He gets up and begins pacing the room. "For Christ's sake, can't anything go my way?" He leans against the wall, breathing heavily.

"If he's dead," Frej says, coming closer, "then it's probably because Gina saw him coming, and she shot him. If he's not … then that's even worse. It means they joined forces. And they're probably plotting against us right now."

"He wouldn't do that," Fritz mutters, staring at the wall. "He loves his son. Jeopardizing the life of his newborn, that's insane. Believe me, I know. No father would do such a thing."

"These people *are* insane," Frej says. "They've proven that plenty of times. They're unstable, unpredictable. I have a bad feeling, Dad. I think we need to plan for the worst."

Fritz turns to look up at his son. Almost two full feet taller than Fritz now, his clothes can no longer hide his meaty chest or the wiry muscles of his arms and legs.

He's awesome to look at. In the true sense of the word. And he's not even fully mature yet.

"What do you have in mind?" Fritz asks.

Frej's eyes are gleaming. "I think they might come for us."

"But they don't know where we are."

"I think they do."

"How?"

Frej shrugs. "I don't know, it's just ... a gut feeling. I can't ... what's the word? ... pin them down. Because of Gina. But I can sense they're getting closer."

Fritz swallows. He knows it would be a mistake not to trust Frej's instincts. Not to take it seriously. "When?"

"Soon."

"All right." Fritz nods and looks around the room. "All right. We need to get ready for them, then. But we can't let people know. It'll just scare them."

"Let me deal with them, Dad."

"No!" Fritz turns to Frej and points a finger in his face. He feels silly doing so—like a dwarf telling off a giant. "You're not ready."

Frej nods calmly. "Yes. I am. I will kill them all, Dad."

"You're not immortal, Son," Fritz says, mustering a caring tone. "They can hurt you. They can even kill you."

"They won't get the chance," Frej says, speaking with all the self-confidence of a teenager ready to take on the world. "I'm too fast. Too strong. I will tear them apart before they see me coming. Let me show you what I can do, Dad."

Fritz considers it despite himself. He knows Frej is probably right. The boy killed a man minutes after being born. But he's still Fritz's responsibility. At least a little while longer. And he hates running unnecessary risks.

"Listen to me, Son," he says, taking Frej by the arms. "You will get to prove yourself to me and to the world. But there's no rush.

These people ... they're vermin. They're not worth the risk, or even the effort. You are meant to rule, my son. And you will. But let me deal with Gina and Hoffman and whoever else they've convinced to join them. If they really are coming, they're in for a rude surprise. We outnumber them by a great margin."

"But, Dad," Frej says intently. "I really want to do this."

"I know, Son. I promise you, next time. For now, I'll get the men ready, have them take up positions around the base. As soon as we spot them, we'll take them down."

Frej imitates a sigh. "All right. But you promise, next time ...?"

"Next time," Fritz says.

13
ALICIA

She's sitting cross-legged on the ground. Using a stick, she prods a big spider this way then that, making it scurry around in circles.

She's barely aware that she's humming the nursery rhyme her mother used to sing at bedtime. Only she has altered the text slightly.

"Itsy bitsy spider trying to get away. Down came the stick, and blocked its little way. Running, running, all the livelong day. The itsy bitsy spider will never get away."

Her mother never liked spiders. In fact, she hated them. Whenever one appeared in the house, she would freak out. If it was tiny, she might kill it with a fly swatter. But for anything bigger than a fingernail, she would call Grandpa. He lived just a few blocks over, and he didn't mind popping by. He never killed the spiders, though. Instead, he caught them using a glass and a piece of paper, then gently let them out into the garden. Mom hated that he did this. She claimed they would just find their way back inside. But she could never get Grandpa to kill them.

Alicia is much more like Grandpa. She never minded spiders either, and she also didn't want them dead. Once her mother learned that Alicia wasn't afraid of the tiny creatures, she made her get rid of them instead so they didn't need to bother Grandpa.

Alicia misses Grandpa. Misses him so much that just thinking about him makes her heart hurt. Not as much as when she first came here. But still enough for a sob to catch in her throat. She focuses on the spider and resumes humming.

She's so caught up in the game, she doesn't hear the boy coming around the truck before he bumps into her, kneeing her on the shoulder, almost tipping her over.

"Ouch!" she exclaims, whacking him with the stick. "Watch out, idiot!"

The guy is carrying two big metal cases, one in each hand. She realizes too late who he is. Not that she cares all that much. But she knows the guy has a reputation as one of the Prophet's favorites, so she probably shouldn't have struck him.

The Bomber doesn't seem to be hurt, though. He's staring at her in surprise. "Alicia?" he asks.

Hearing her old name, it stirs something inside of her. Just like when Camilla said it. And when Mark said it. And whenever she thinks it out loud inside her head. It's not very pleasant. It feels like something is trying to wake up deep down in her belly, something big and powerful. Like a sleeping dragon. She doesn't understand what it is exactly, but she much prefers it to stay asleep.

"That's not my name anymore," she murmurs. "I'm the Poppy now."

"Yeah, all right, whatever," he says, darting a look around, then lowering his voice. "But you're the one who took the baby, right?"

She squints up at him. "Yeah, so?"

The guy opens his mouth as though to tell her something. Then he seems to think better of it. "Nothing," he says. "Never mind. Watch out."

Stepping past her, he crushes the spider under his heel without even noticing, leaving it as a gooey mass with black, twitching legs.

She glares after him, pissed that he ruined her game. She'll have to go find another spider now, and that could take hours.

Watching the guy leave, another idea occurs to her. She's been bored ever since bringing back the baby. She doesn't have a job like the others, so she basically just hangs around all day, trying to make time pass. The way the Bomber walks, darting quick glances around, she gets the feeling he's up to something. Something which is probably much more exciting than teasing spiders.

Alicia waits until he's just out of sight. Then she gets up and quickly follows him.

14

MARK

Under normal conditions, it's a three-hour drive—assuming they avoid rush hour.

But with tons of cars either crashed, or simply left haphazardly in the middle of the road, they are looking at more like double that time.

It's not everywhere the roads are impassable; for long stretches, there are no obstacles at all. This is especially true when they're out in the open landscape between cities. However, as soon as another town comes up ahead, vehicles, dead bodies and other things begin to clutter their way, and they have to slow down and go in zigzag. Since they make sure to follow the freeway around the cities rather than going through them, they hardly meet anyone alive. Now and then, they'll see lone drifters or smaller groups of blind people, but they are easily left in the dust.

The most difficult parts are the bridges. Going from Zealand to Jutland, they need to cross the Great and then the Little Belt Bridge, and just as Mark feared, both overpasses are clogged with cars trying to get off the islands. Luckily, it seems like someone else—probably military—have come along after the fact and made a narrow passage by pushing cars out of the way. There's broken glass everywhere, and some of the smaller vehicles have been tipped onto their sides. In a few places, they need to utilize the truck's horsepower and shove aside a car that's still blocking the way.

It's not easy, but they make it onto the mainland and head north.

Nick drove the first fifty miles, then Gina took over, and now Mark is behind the wheel. He keeps checking the clock on the dashboard. Looks like they'll make it just in time.

His mind is weirdly focused. It should be freaking out, or at the very least gearing up. But even though his thoughts circle around Danny a lot, he's able to stay calm and clear inside. The fear is there, of course, but it simply doesn't hold enough sway over him to sweep him away.

"I'm never letting him out of sight again."

Mark turns his head to look at Camilla. She was nodding off earlier, but now she's sitting upright, staring at the road ahead.

"He's going to stay within three feet of me until he's twenty-one."

Mark smiles. "That'll be awkward when he finds a girl."

"I don't care," Camilla says. "I'm not taking any more chances."

"We didn't take a chance," Mark says. "We were sleeping. The front door was locked. There was absolutely no way of predicting that would happen."

Camilla sighs deeply. "I can't help thinking if I'd just waited to go to the bathroom. Or maybe woken you up first. Then maybe—"

"They would have found a way," Mark says. "Evil always does. Don't blame yourself, Camilla. The girl obviously planned it out.

She wanted you to scream out for me, so she could slip past me and take him."

Camilla squeezes her lips together and nods. "I'm really scared he won't be OK. Or that we won't get him back."

"Yeah, me too." He reaches over and takes her hand. "We'll just have to stay strong for him."

There's a brief pause. Mark checks the mirror. It's dark in the back, but he can make out their silhouettes. John and Lisa both appear to be resting, the girl leaning against her dad. Nick is slumped over too, and even Gina has leaned back her head and seems to be asleep.

The only figure still awake is Anton. He's staring ahead, apparently at nothing, while caressing the dog, who's sitting between his legs.

Poor guy. Probably thinking of his brother.

Mark can't imagine what it would be like, losing your twin. Someone who's always been right by your side. Your best friend. And at such a young age.

Fate certainly didn't pull any punches. It was obviously just as gruesome to kids as it was to adults.

"I can't help feeling bad for her," Camilla says, as though reading Mark's thoughts. "Alicia. She was just so … I mean, her eyes … I could barely recognize her."

Mark swallows. "Yeah. Gina said the same about Tommy. Those fucking ghosts really do a number on you if you cave."

"I hope she's OK," Camilla says, glancing out the side window as they pass a house that's recently been burned to the ground. "I hope she's not in too much pain."

Mark considers. "Do you think she can be saved? Do you think any of them can?"

"You mean if we kill that thing? I'm not sure. From what that guy told Gina ... it sounds like this is much bigger than we knew. If there are really thousands of them all over the globe, then ..."

"Yeah, I know, but ... what if it's like ... localized in this creature? Like a thorn. Pull it out, and the inflammation goes down."

"What about the ghosts? Alicia would still have to face her mother."

"I guess so. But without this evil energy, it might be considerably easier."

Camilla thinks this over. "I guess it's plausible. I think Gina is right in that the ghosts are really nothing more than our personal trauma brought to the surface and put on steroids. What could have been dealt with through therapy and over a long time is suddenly being thrust upon us. We're forced to face it, and it's either sink or swim. There's no in-between. But I also think it's never too late to swim, you know? There's always another chance. I mean, no matter how depressed or scared or guilt-ridden you feel, it's always possible to find your way back. Even badly damaged minds can heal. It just takes a long time and a lot of effort." She takes a deep breath. "So, yeah. I think there's hope for Alicia and the others. At least I really hope so."

Mark nods slowly. "I hope so, too. And I guess we'll find out for sure soon enough. Because that glow out there ..." He points towards the horizon. "I believe that's the airbase. We'll arrive right on time. Better wake up the others and get them ready."

15
TOMMY

There's a big concrete box in the middle of the airstrip. About twelve feet tall, it has a metal hatch and several antennas. It's probably some kind of tech center. Tommy doesn't care what it's for; it's the perfect spot. Open to all sides, it has a clear view of the row of trees to the south.

The concrete will provide him bulletproof coverage, in case they begin firing back at him, which he assumes they will. The only thing missing is an escape route. Sitting out in the open, Tommy can't make a run for it if he needs to. Which means he can only dig in and keep shooting.

It's all good, though. He knows he probably won't walk away from this alive. He's come to terms with that. As long as he can set this right. If he can just complete his final task. Finish what he started. Then he can die in peace.

He waits till he can hear everyone around him snoring. The only exception is the Twin. Lying in the bunk next to him, she's resting with one hand behind her head, staring up at underside of the top bunk. Tommy lies on his side, watching her carefully through narrow eyes. Now and then, she'll turn her head to glance over at him, and Tommy will pretend to be fast asleep.

Come on, Tommy thinks, feeling impatient. *It's time. Just get up.*

And finally, the girl does so. She slips out of bed and leaves so quietly, Tommy almost misses it. He realizes he was drifting off for a moment, because suddenly, the bunk next to him is empty. Sitting up abruptly, he leans over and looks towards the exit. He just catches glimpse of the door closing, cutting off the moonlight.

He immediately gets dressed, pulling on his clothes with shaky hands. Then he leaves the barracks, closing the door gently. He looks over at the hangar, where the lights are on. He can hear faint bustling from the night shifters. Tommy slips around the corner of the building and starts running.

It's a long way out there. He's completely exposed all the way, but the sun has dipped below the horizon, and the half-moon and the stars only cast a bluish glow that's probably not enough for any casual onlookers to see him jog across the lot—even if anyone was looking, which he finds highly unlikely.

A few minutes later, he reaches the post, stopping to catch his breath. The summer night is humid, and he's sweating under the black clothes.

"I'll need a shower after this," he grunts. Then—realizing just how absurd that thought is—he almost bursts out laughing. He won't need a shower after this, because there will be no "after this." Not for him, anyway. And, if he does the job right, not for Gina, either.

Tommy glances up at the broken sky. The unearthly glow is coming through the cracks. He'll never get used to it; it's beautiful and frightening at the same time.

All right, get to work. It must be close to midnight.

He looks over at the pines. They rock gently in the mild night breeze. No vehicles, figures or lights in sight.

Tommy walks around the concrete block and sees the metal boxes where he left them. He really didn't find it likely that anyone would come all the way out here to find them, but he still made his way past the mechanic shop where they were working on a plane, and he managed to find two small padlocks in a cabinet full of different tools.

Crouching, he dials the combination on the first box, opening it to reveal the ammo.

Then he takes the bigger case—but then hesitates. The digits are wrong. He remembers leaving the lock at 1-2-3-4, but now it's a random number.

Tommy frowns. Someone tried to open it.

As though the thought makes it happen, someone grunts nearby.

Tommy leans sideways to look around to the other side of the block.

On the ground lies the redheaded girl, curled up, arms wrapped around herself, sleeping.

"What the hell?" Tommy blurts out. "What are *you* doing here?"

16

NORA

Nora knows the boy isn't sleeping. His eyes are closed, but his breathing is way too even. He's also not thrusting, turning or muttering. For some reason, he's only pretending. Maybe he's just not tired.

Whatever the case, Nora can't leave with him noticing, so she waits patiently.

Lying in her bunk, she thinks of Nick. She recalls his face on the phone. His eyes. They were so alive. Just hours ago, she had been convinced he was still lying in the hotel room, rotting away.

Seeing him, talking to him, knowing that he is safe and well, it made her feel like her old self again—only even more so. She's somehow different from the Nora she was back before this whole thing began. The young woman living alone in a cozy flat downtown, studying to become a grade-school teacher, dating a nondescript guy named Thomas who was very sweet despite still staying with his parents.

This new Nora is much older, much wiser, but at the same time, she's also paradoxically younger. Or rather, age-less.

She can feel the darkness. It's certainly still there. And, after having returned to the barracks, she feels it more acutely. It's definitely this place. It might not be producing the darkness—she suspects that's really inside of her—but it's certainly amplifying it. Nora is convinced that anybody staying here for too long will forever succumb to their inner demons, and likely never recover. She's very grateful that she'll only need to stay for a little while longer.

She has already decided that she's making a run for it, no matter what happens. Like Steffie, Nora understands the huge risk involved in betraying this place, betraying Fritz and the monster he calls his son. She needs only think of the poor Bouncer. He made just a minor mistake, yet he was tortured to death. There was no telling what punishment Fritz would lay upon them if he caught them trying to free Danny and run away with him. Perhaps he would simply feed them all to his son.

Rumors were starting to go around. About what Fritz needed all those dead bodies for. Why they were never seen again. And what was in the bags that got hauled out the back.

Cannibal. That's the word Nora has heard whispered more than once. And, having seen the creature—Frej, as Fritz announced he would be known as—Nora isn't exactly surprised. When he's just standing still, looking neutral, he could maybe pass for a human being, a very tall and gangly teenager. At least at a passing glance. But as soon as he moves, talks or makes any facial expressions, the illusion shatters.

It has the mouth of a predator. The mannerisms of a sociopath. The eyes of a dead soul.

It's a monster, clean and simple.

Nora saw it before, but she for some reason bought what Fritz was saying anyway. That Frej was just as human as everyone else—in fact, even more so. He was the future of mankind, the one who would save their species from inevitable demise, pull them from the brink of extinction and instead lead them into a new era, humanity's golden age.

It sounded wonderful. It was met with cheers and tears and something close to hysteria.

She saw it before, but now Nora *really* sees it. There's nothing human about the creature. It's a mask. And a thin, unconvincing one at that. Its intentions are not benign at all. It's not come to save them, but to eradicate them.

And it scares her. The thought of these creatures being born all over the world ... it's a whole new level of danger. The blind people are only people, and they eventually die of hunger and exhaustion.

These things, on the other hand, they have plenty to eat, and Nora doesn't think it likely they'll be easy to kill.

She realizes her thoughts are turning dark again, and she forces the image of her brother back into her mind. It immediately brightens her outlook. She's still scared, still worried, but she's not overwhelmed. She's able to act.

Glancing sideways, she can tell the boy is finally asleep—or at least close to it. His mouth is ajar, and his forehead is slightly creased.

She immediately pulls the blanket aside and slips out of bed. She remembers to bring the small package she has hidden under the pillow. She's already wearing her full outfit, including shoes, so she heads right for the door, making sure to move swiftly and silently. Checking her watch, she finds that it's twenty to twelve.

I need to hurry.

She runs along the building, staying close to the wall. There's light in the hangar, but no one is outside at this hour.

Reaching the corner of the barrack, she glances out over the lot—and then immediately retracts her head again, as a group of men is standing not far away, smoking and chatting. They're armed with heavy guns.

What the hell?

There's usually no guards around. Everyone here is free to leave if they want to—which nobody wants to—and there's no real danger of any intruders coming to attack them, since no one knew about this place. And even if they did, who in their right mind would lay siege to an airbase with several thousand people and just as many guns available?

Nora stays perfectly still and listens to the men's conversation. They're talking in low voices, obviously not wanting to be heard.

"Really should be catching some z's right now."

"Don't see the point in this fucking show."

"The hell anyone's coming. Betcha we ain't seeing nothin'."

"Better keep your eyes open anyway."

"Yeah, last thing you want is the Prophet popping by to see you nodding off. You heard him. He wasn't playin' around."

Nora slips back the other way, feeling her heart rate rise even higher.

Fritz knows they're coming. He's told these guys to keep guard.

Ducking, she runs to the next barrack, slipping into the shadows. Her mind is reeling. Did anyone overhear her conversation with the group? Did Steffie tell on them?

No, it made no sense. If either of those were the case, then Fritz would know exactly where to expect them. He wouldn't bother putting up a group of men next to the sleeping barracks.

And besides, someone would have come for Nora already and taken her to see Fritz for her punishment.

Perhaps he's just grown paranoid. Could just be a precaution.

But Nora doubts it. She doesn't think Fritz knows exactly what's going to happen, but he must have a feeling that *something* is going on. He has a way of knowing things without having heard them stated outright. Like how he knew about her and Nick's bond. How he was able to drop in at the exact right time and place, just as Nora was about to bludgeon Steffie to death.

He's hearing voices. Someone's guiding him. Telling him things in advance.

Nora knows this is serious. It means they need to be extra careful. And the worst part is, she has no way of warning the others, because she didn't dare bring her phone back to the barracks, so she left it in the house with Steffie.

She has made it around the second barrack, and stops briefly by the corner to catch her breath. Scanning the airstrip, she doesn't see any other groups of gunmen. At least no one that's standing around. But she does see a jeep that's parked near a lone antenna a fair distance out. Its engine is off, but it somehow looks out of place.

Staring at it, Nora catches a movement through the windows. Someone is in there. She's willing to bet a lot of money it's more gunmen.

Another post. Ready to shoot at anyone who shows up uninvited.

Nora feels a cold shiver run down her sweaty back. She needs to reach Steffie and Danny as quickly as she can. She needs to get to her phone, call Nick and warn them. Maybe they need to postpone the whole thing. Maybe it's too risky.

Nora looks over at the office building. It's out in the open, and she'll have no cover whatsoever. She'll have to just go for it. Hoping whoever is in the jeep doesn't check the mirrors for the next thirty seconds or so.

Nora hyperventilates a few times, bringing in extra oxygen. Then she bolts.

17
FRITZ

He should be sleeping. He's certainly tired enough. But he can't. Not now. Not until this is over.

Because Gina is coming. He doesn't know when or where. But she will show up, and he needs to be ready. It could be the chance he was hoping for. It could all end tonight.

He saunters back and forth in the basement. It's incredibly beautiful down here. Had he found out sooner, he'd have made this his office instead. He just might still do that. He could even make it his retirement home. Because as soon as the fighting is over, Frej will leave the nest to go out into the world, and Fritz will no longer serve a useful purpose. His job will be done.

The others—all the minions upstairs, busy building a war machine—will still be needed, because there are others like Gina and her gang out there, and they will need to be wiped out before the new world can be built.

And speaking of building a new world—the basement was made decades ago by people wanting to do just that: create a vastly different future, a future in which a particular race ruled superior. He read from the framed sign on the wall that the basement has been kept almost completely as it looked during the occupation. There are even still swastikas in the tile patterns of the bathroom—which also had a vomitorium, designed for when the Nazi officers went at it a bit too hard and needed to puke up some of the undoubtedly delicious meals they were served.

Fritz can feel a strong atmosphere down here. It's like the spirits of the previous occupants are still here. *This is the real reason why I chose this place. I had no idea this wonderful basement was here all along, right below. But I could sense it.*

In a way, he has done what the Nazis failed to do. He has set into motion the machinery that'll actually change the world. He's made it possible. And soon he can step back and watch it all unfold, knowing that none of it could have come about without his—

The heavy double doors burst open like they're made of cardboard, slamming into the brick walls.

Fritz spins around to see Frej standing there. Breathing fast, his chest expands and contracts rapidly. He's too tall to stand upright, and his eyes are fixed on Fritz.

"What is it?" Fritz asks, already knowing the answer.

"They're coming," Frej whispers.

18
TOMMY

The girl sits up with a start and looks around. The Alice band drops from her hair, and her head whips this way then that, until she finally sees him. She swallows and blinks. "Uhm ... hey."

"What the fuck are you doing here?" Tommy demands again, bending down to grab the girl's shirt. He lifts her to her feet and stares at her. "Why are you here? Gina send you? Huh? Did she?"

"What? No! Who's Gina? I'm just ... Let go of me!"

She tears free by pushing Tommy back, and they glare at each other for a moment.

"Why are you here?" Tommy snarls.

"Why are *you* here?" the girl retorts, picking up her hairband with a snappy movement. She whips her hair back and puts the band back in.

"That's none of your damn business," Tommy says, pointing at her. "You've been meddling with my stuff. So you better tell me what you're doing here and how you found me, or I'll kick your ass. I don't care that you're a girl."

"Uuh, scary," the Poppy sneers. "You just try!"

Tommy lowers his voice. "You know I've killed people, right?"

The girl's eyes flicker only briefly. Then she pulls out a knife from her back pocket. Tommy can tell it's a steak knife she got in the cantina. The blade is serrated and will no doubt leave a nasty scar if she cuts him with it. He decides she's not worth the energy.

"I'm not wasting any more time on you," Tommy sneers, turning his back on her. "Do whatever the hell you want. I've got more important business."

He unlocks the box and takes out the machine gun. There's a wide-legged tripod stand and several other parts that need to be assembled. He goes to work.

The girl peers around the corner. "What's that?"

Tommy glances over at her. She's still holding the knife. "It's a giant dildo," he mumbles. "What does it look like?"

"It looks like a gun."

"No fooling you," Tommy says, clicking the scope into place. "Now, please leave."

"Who are you gonna shoot with it?"

Tommy doesn't answer.

The Poppy just keeps standing there, watching him put the gun together.

"If I tell you how I found you, will you tell who you plan to shoot?" she asks. Her tone is less confrontational now. More curious.

Tommy grunts. "You know I could just shoot you, right?"

"Yeah, but you're not going to," the Poppy says defiantly. "Because you don't want anyone to know you're out here."

Tommy bites down hard. He's almost done. He just needs the ammo, so he takes the other box.

"I followed you," the girl says simply. "After you stepped on my spider."

"Your what?"

"After you bumped into me. Behind the truck. Earlier today."

"Oh."

She shrugs. "I just snuck after you. I saw you get the padlocks, then you came all the way out there. I watched you from over there ..." She points at the trees. "When you left, I came over here to see what you'd hidden. When I couldn't get the box open, I decided to wait. I knew you'd probably come back soon, but I must've fallen asleep."

"You're one Nosey Nelly," Tommy grumbles.

"Well, can I stay?"

He sighs. He doesn't really see the harm. The girl sticking around is probably better than her going back to the hangar, where she might tell someone about Tommy being out here.

"If you don't bug me," he says. "And keep quiet."

"Sure, no problem!" The girl actually smiles as she slips the steak knife back into her pocket. She comes to stand next to him. "So, who are we shooting at?"

Tommy raises one eyebrow. "This is your idea of 'quiet'?"

"Just tell me, and I'll shut up. Promise. But I need to know who we're killing, right?"

Tommy gives her a long look. Her pale face against the black night sky is for some reason disturbing. Maybe it's the eager look in her eyes.

She's really messed up. Been here for too long.

"*We* aren't killing anyone," he tells her. "I am."

"Is it that woman you mentioned? What was it, Dina?"

"Gina."

"Right. Is that her? What did she do to you?"

"Nothing. She just needs to die, that's all."

"But why?"

"Because she's dangerous. And ... it's my job. The Prophet told me to do it."

This isn't technically true, but it does finally make the girl shut up for a while. The real reason he's doing this is because he knows it's what Fritz wants. Or, rather, what the powers that he represents want. They acted through the memory of his father before, gently guiding him, but now, Tommy is on his own. It should have been finished, but he fumbled on the finish line—those fucking batteries, if he hadn't forgotten to put them in, Gina would be toast—and now he needs to finish what he started.

If I don't, I'll never be free.

The guilt is too much. Tommy wants it to go away, just like Fritz promised him, and now he understands why it's still lingering. Because he didn't do his job properly. He didn't finish it.

Tommy checks that everything is in order. He doesn't know much about actual guns, but he has played a few video games. He's pretty confident the gun is ready to fire. He lifts the whole thing—it's surprisingly heavy—and places it close up against the concrete block, the barrel aimed at the tree line.

"When is she coming?" the Poppy asks.

"Midnight. Over there. By the pines."

"Will she come alone? Or will—"

"Shut up!"

Tommy hisses at the girl as he picks up on a sound. It's an engine approaching. A big one. It sounds like it's still far away, but the breeze is carrying the sound. Tommy drops to his stomach and grabs the gun. It's only now he realizes that he didn't adjust the height properly, and he begins fumbling with the stand.

"Tell me if you see a truck," he whispers.

The girl nods and looks at the trees, squinting as she strains her eyes.

Tommy listens as the engine comes slowly closer, and he manages to get the gun lowered a few inches. He fastens the screws and takes the right position—or what he assumes is the right position, going on what soldiers do in the movies.

"There!" the girl says, pointing. "I see it!"

Tommy follows her finger and makes out the outline of the truck. It's stopped close to the end of the tree line, engine idling, lights off, and it's hard to make out if it wasn't for the sound of the engine.

"Now what?" the girl whispers, crouching down next to Tommy.

"Now you cover your ears," he mutters, closing one eye to look through the scope.

He sees the trees and the truck behind them, but it's out of focus. He finds the button and turns it back and forth until the image is sharp.

He can see the guy behind the wheel—it's a young, skinny dude with a buzz-cut he never saw before. He didn't hear him talking over the phone, either, so it could be someone new. He turns around in his seat and apparently says something to someone in the back. He uses his hands a lot when he talks.

Is that sign language? Is he deaf?

Tommy swings the scope and the gun slightly to the right, finding the back of the truck. The door swings open, and a man jumps out. His clothes are different, but Tommy immediately recognizes him.

"Hey, Mark," he mutters.

"Mark?" the girl repeats, her voice sharp.

Tommy shushes her sharply. "Keep it down! They'll hear us."

"Did you say 'Mark'?" the Poppy repeats, lowering her voice slightly. "Who are these people?"

Tommy looks at her briefly. "They're the parents of the baby you stole."

The girl slaps a hand across her mouth, her eyes going big and round. "Why ... why are they here?"

"To get back their baby, of course," Tommy mutters, placing his eye against the ocular again. "And they brought the woman I need to kill."

A movement from the side catches his eye.

Across the lot comes the Twin. She's running. In her arms is a bundle wrapped in a blanket. Tommy can hear her shoes against the concrete, can hear her heave for breath, can hear the baby whimpering as it's being bobbed up and down.

"Jesus," the Poppy whispers. "That's her ... and she brought Danny ..."

Tommy ignores her. He swerves back to the truck. Mark has come through the trees now. He's looking through a pair of binoculars, scanning his surroundings. Someone else is there, too. A young woman Tommy doesn't know. She runs towards the Twin, her face a mask of fear and relief.

Must be the baby's mother. Come on, Gina. Where are you?

And then he sees her. She emerges from between the pines. She tricked him by moving farther down the tree line, closer to the hangar. She's holding a gun and looking very alert.

Tommy feels his pulse rise. His finger finds the trigger. The Poppy says something, but he filters it out completely.

Stop moving, Gina. Just stay still for half a second.

Gina is shifting back and forth, taking a few steps this way, then that. Almost like she knows someone is taking aim at her, and she doesn't want to get pinned down.

Then she finally stops. And she looks right at Tommy. Except she probably can't see him—it must be the concrete block she's looking at.

It doesn't matter either way.

Tommy's got her.

19
NORA

It feels like crossing the airstrip takes forever, even though she's sprinting at full speed.

For every step, she fears hearing someone shout for her. Or worse, a gun going off.

But that doesn't happen.

Reaching the building, she almost slams against the wall. Stepping around the corner, she collapses to her hands and knees and heaves for breath. As she's finally able to breathe regularly again, she gets up and glances back towards the jeep. It's still just sitting there. No one is coming out. No lights have been turned on.

I made it. They didn't see me.

She slinks around the building, going for the door, when—

She stops abruptly and jumps back. One more step, and she would have tripped over a fat guy sitting on the ground, back leaning against the wall, mouth open, snoring away. Across his lap is a rifle, and on the ground next to him is a flashlight and a large, steel thermos bottle.

Nora doesn't dare breathe, so she holds it in as she steps around the guy. He seems to be sound asleep, but she can't take any chances. Turning the knob, she finds the door locked. She taps it gently, keeping a close eye on the guard. If he opens his eyes, she'll go for his rifle.

"Yes?" Steffie's voice from the other side, very low.

"It's me," Nora whispers.

The door is immediately unlocked and opened. Nora steps in, and Steffie shuts and locks the door after her. Turning around, the girl looks at her with big, scared eyes. "He was here earlier. The Prophet. He knows something is up."

Nora nods. "I could tell from the guards."

"He said they might be coming for Danny," Steffie goes on, going to the bed. "That I had to be extra watchful. And that if I saw or heard anything, I was to scream out as loud as I could." She gently wraps Danny in another blanket as she keeps talking. "You really need to go right now. If he comes back and sees you here, he'll kill both of us." She picks up Danny. "Please, just take him and go."

"All right," Nora says. "Let me just check." She quickly pulls out the package from the back of her pants and puts it on the bed. A sudden impulse makes her cover it with the blanket.

Then, she strides to the narrow window facing south. The airstrip is open and empty under the pale moonlight. The pines are visible in the distance. It'll be a long run. Ten times as long as the one she just did. And she'll once again be completely exposed the entire way. Plus, she'll be running with the baby in her arms.

"Please, Nora," Steffie says, sounding like she's about to cry. "He might come back any moment."

Nora goes to take the baby. In order to do so, she steps around the bed. And that's when she hears the doorknob rattle. The lock snaps open.

Steffie gasps and spins around. Nora looks towards the door, seeing it start to open, and then she ducks down behind the bed. She stares at the boots coming through the opening. They stop just inside.

"Hello, Junkie," Fritz's voice comes. Nora can tell right away he sounds different. He's not talking with his usual smug coolness. Instead, there's tension in his voice. Perhaps even a hint of fear. "I wanted to check on you. Is the baby OK?"

"He's … fine," Steffie says, the words catching in her throat. She's standing by the head of the bed, and Nora wants her badly to step closer to Fritz, so that he in turn won't come closer to the bed. But Steffie seems nailed to the spot. "I just fed him, and … and I was about to tuck him in."

"Good," Fritz says. His feet shift a little, first to the left, then to the right. As though he's turning his body to scan the room. "That's good. And you haven't seen anyone?"

"No," Steffie answers way too fast. "No one."

A brief pause. Then Fritz comes closer to Steffie and the bed. Nora notices the door is still open, showing what looks like a basement. She sends up a silence prayer, thanking God that she decided at the last second to cover the package, or Fritz would no doubt have seen it.

"Let me see him," Fritz says. He doesn't sound affectionate, like he's dying to lay eyes on the cute little face, but more like someone who's forced to look at something they find off-putting.

"He's ... he's sleeping," Steffie says, her voice very thin now.

"Just a quick look," Fritz tells her, stopping right in front of Steffie.

Nora holds her breath. Her pulse is going so hard, she can feel it behind her eyeballs. She can't crawl under the bed, because it's not tall enough, and the naked springs look like they'll give off loud noises if she as much as touches them.

"See?" Steffie says. "He's sleeping. Just like I said."

"Yes," Fritz says. "I can tell. Don't you think the extra blanket is a bit much? It seems warm enough in here."

"I guess you're right," Steffie mutters. She unwraps the blanket and drops it on the bed. "There. Better?"

Fritz seems about to answer, when Nora catches a movement from the open doorway. Turning her head, she sees a couple of huge, bare feet come striding through. The legs are bare, too, at least halfway up the shins, where the pant legs begin.

If Nora couldn't tell who just entered the room with them, Steffie's gasp gives it away.

"I told you to wait, Frej," Fritz says, turning around.

"But, Dad, I can help." The creature's voice is deeper, booming almost, but still somewhat scratchy, like that of a big teenager. "They're very close. I can feel it."

"I'm taking care of it. Please, go back."

The creature doesn't go. Instead, it steps farther into the room, seemingly looking around. "Someone's playing us, Dad. Someone's helping them."

A long, silent pause. Everyone seems to hold their breath.

Then Fritz says: "You seem very nervous, Junkie. Is my son scaring you? There's no need to be afraid. He won't harm you."

Nora gets ready to jump up and run. She'll make a dash for the door. She probably won't make it, but it's her only chance.

"No, it's just ... this whole situation," Steffie croaks. She's obviously fighting not to cry now. "It's very ... scary. I hope nothing happens to the baby."

That last sentence sounds genuine, and Fritz seems to buy that that's the real reason for Steffie's anxiety, because when he speaks again, he sounds less accusatory. "I understand. You and the baby are both safe here. The guard is right outside, and no one's coming in here. I assure you ..." Something seems to catch Fritz's eye, because he turns towards the bed and trails off. "Hmm."

"What?" Steffie blurts out, alarm in her voice. "What is it?"

Nora's mind is running a thousand miles an hour. Has Fritz caught her scent? Did she make a noise she wasn't aware of? Did she leave anything on the bed that he has noticed? She can't think of what that would be, but—

"That window over there," Fritz says, starting to move around the bed. "We might need to get someone to board it up. Just to be on the safe side."

Nora follows his feet as he comes closer. She ducks down farther, trying to make herself invisible. But she's not. In fact, she's lying in clear view, and Fritz is only three steps away. Instead, she readies herself to jump up and run.

"Prophet!" Steffie cries out.

He stops and turns. "What's wrong?"

"The ... the guard," Steffie wheezes, audibly pushing out the words now. "The man you ... placed outside ..."

"Yes?"

"He's sleeping. You told him to ... to stay awake, but ... he's snoring away."

Fritz's voice changes. "I hope that's not true."

"It is!" Steffie insists. "Go have a look for yourself. Please."

Fritz hesitates for a moment, then strides to the door. Closing it, he opens it again right away. This time, the opening shows the proper view: the dark, open lot.

"Come on, Frej," Fritz says. He steps outside and goes to the left, where the guy is sitting. The creature follows him willingly. Fritz closes the door after them, then says loudly: "Are you kidding me, Snowman?"

A grunt of surprise. Someone begins babbling, and Fritz threatens to have the guy torn to shreds. The guy pleads for his life, saying something about coffee and sleep apnea.

Nora only listens with half an ear. The moment Fritz closed the door, she jumped to her feet and went for the window. She has opened it all the way, and is frantically waving Steffie closer. She has already caught on, and she comes over with Danny. Nora hoists herself up, climbs out and jumps down. Steffie reaches the bundle out the window, and Nora catches a glimpse of Danny's face as she takes him in her arms.

She sends Steffie one last look. The girl's eyes are beaming with fear, but also a modicum of relief. "Go," she whispers. "Get him to safety."

"Thank you," Nora says—it's all she can think of.

Then she turns and runs, headed for the ragged shadows in the distance, which she knows are the trees.

After two hundred yards or so, a piercing scream cuts through the night.

Nora can't help but slow down and dart a look back. Another scream, even louder and more shrill. This time it's full of pain. It's coming from inside the building she just left. And it can only be Steffie. Then the scream is cut off abruptly, followed by dead silence.

Nora runs even faster.

20
GINA

She steps through the branches and looks around the airstrip. It's even bigger than she imagined.

Off in the distance are the main buildings—the hangar that Nora told them about, flanked by the barracks. The lights are on in the former.

Closer by is a minor building, which she assumes must be where they kept Danny, because it's from that direction she sees Nora come running, clutching a bundle against her chest.

As Camilla runs out to meet her, Gina sees Mark farther down the tree line. He catches her eye and sends her a brief nod, signaling that he hasn't seen anyone.

Gina looks around again, and this time, she notices a concrete block not that far off. It's shaped like a building, but it's too small, so it's probably more like a tech box of some kind. For some reason, her attention is drawn to it, and her eyes linger there for a moment. She gets a feeling—almost like a sixth sense—that someone over there is looking back at her. She can't see anything but shadows, but she's almost certain that—

Suddenly, everything is bathed in a sharp light, as huge floodlights just overhead are turned on, along with others standing farther away.

Gina blinks and shields her eyes.

Her first thought is that Nora tricked them. Lured them into a trap.

But then she sees Nora handing over Danny to Camilla, and both women head for the tree line.

Then comes the ear-piercing sound of a siren blaring. It's very much like those air raid drills the military will run once every year, except Gina has never heard it this close before. She spins around, looking out over the airstrip, and she feels her heart sink. Three—no four—sets of headlights are coming right for them from different directions. She can't tell for sure, but it looks like jeeps.

This is a trap.

She turns to shout at Mark, but he's already seen the oncoming vehicles. So, she ducks and runs for the trees, seeing Camilla and Nora squeeze through.

"*Mom!*"

Anton's voice, coming from the back of the truck. Gina sees him, leaning out the door, holding on with one hand. With the other, he's pointing out over the field. Gina follows his finger and sees two more headlights coming this way, cutting off the road they just came from.

Damnit. We're surrounded.

Nora helps Camilla into the truck, then looks back at Gina. "Come on! What are you waiting for?"

Mark comes running. "Shit, this is bad. We've got no choice but to cross the airstrip."

"I know," Gina says. "Tell Nick. I'll cover you."

"*What?*" Anton cries out, as Gina begins backing towards the trees again. "Are you staying? No, Mom, that's suicide!"

"We have no choice, Anton!" she shouts, sending him a significant look. "They're coming. Go now, or we will all die!"

Anton looks like he's about to jump down, when Mark steps in front of him and pushes him into the truck.

Gina looks in the direction of the headlights. They're coming fast. She can hear the roar of the engines over the sirens. She runs to the trees. They'll provide some cover for her, at least initially, but she holds no illusions that she'll be able to survive for long. Whoever are in those vehicles are most certainly coming to kill them, and they're likely armed to the teeth.

As the truck lunges forward, she hears Anton scream for her again, and the sound of his voice is heart-wrenching, but she pushes it firmly aside, focusing instead on the jeeps coming across the open lot. One of them is already here. Locking its brakes, it stops right in front of the concrete block, and five guys dressed in black jump out, all holding guns. They point towards the truck, which is making its way to the end of tree line. In a matter of seconds, it'll come into view, and the men will have a perfect, unobstructed view of it.

Gina crouches, takes aim and is about to shoot, when suddenly, someone beats her to it, opening fire with a succession of loud, rapid bangs.

21

TOMMY

"Ow, it hurts!" Alicia exclaims. "Who turned on all those lights? Did you do that?"

"Of course I didn't," Tommy hisses, rubbing his eyes.

He had her. He had right where he wanted. And then the fucking lights blinded him.

When he's finally able to see again, Gina is gone. On the other side of the tree line, the truck begins moving. In the distance, Tommy can make out two pair of headlights.

They've got them cornered, he realizes, and as he looks back over his shoulder, he sees more vehicles headed for them fast.

He has no idea how Fritz knew Gina and the others were coming, but he obviously did, because this isn't just a random guard sounding the alarm; this is an organized trap. And the truck is caught right in the net. The only two ways are either straight across the airstrip, which means facing the onslaught head-on, or the moor surrounding the airstrip. But while the landscape is open, it's also very uneven and covered in heather and scattered bushes. Even supposing the truck won't get bogged down, the nearest traversable roads are seven miles away. The jeeps will catch up with them long before that.

The girl is still babbling, but Tommy doesn't pay her any attention. His still slightly blurry eyes caught a movement by the trees. It's Gina. She's kneeling, holding her gun. She looks like she's digging in, intending to make a stand and provide the truck with cover, giving the others a chance to get away.

Tommy is about to take aim once again, when a jeep comes in from the side, cutting his view. It stops only a few yards away, and a bunch of men jump out onto the concrete. Tommy recognizes the Vulture. None of them have seen him lying here, right behind them. They're carrying guns—not automatic ones, like Tommy's machine gun, but pretty big ones nonetheless—and they're taking aim at the truck, which is still picking up speed, and is about to come around the end of the tree line in just a few seconds. When it does, the men will no doubt open fire and blow it to pieces.

It'll be like a shooting tent. Only the target is so big, they can't miss it.

Tommy can only stare. He's looking right into the jeep, and his flickering eyes land on the device mounted on the dashboard. Then—

"What's that, Dad?"

—before he's even aware of what he's looking at, a memory—

"It's a GPS, son. It shows me the way."

—comes crashing into his mind. Maybe it's because he's confused and caught completely off guard. Or maybe it's because they're away from the Palace right now. Whatever the reason, Tommy can do nothing to suppress the images coming to life inside his head. He's torn back through time, suddenly only five years old again. He's sitting in a car, driving somewhere with his dad. It's a sunny afternoon, and he's in the front for the first time. It's cool, having a clear view of the road ahead.

"What's that, Dad?" Tommy asks, pointing at the device on the dashboard.

"It's a GPS, son. It shows me the way."

Tommy looks in fascination at the tiny screen as the animated map updates every few seconds, showing the route they're following.

"It works via satellite," his dad says, smiling at Tommy. "Can you believe it?"

"What's a satellite?"

"It's a piece of technology circling the Earth just outside of the atmosphere."

"You mean in outer space?"

"Uh-huh. There are thousands of them up there. This little thing, it receives information from them. Isn't that amazing?"

Tommy leans against the window and squints up at the clear summer sky. A couple of crows glide by, and way up high a plane is drawing a white line, but other than that, he can't see anything.

"They're not visible with the naked eye," his dad explains. "They're too far away and too small. But they're there all right. Sometimes, at night, you can catch a glimpse of one of them. We can try it tonight if you'd like."

"Sure, that'd be cool."

Tommy can't take his eyes off the device. He then notices the word printed on the top corner. It'll be another year until Tommy starts school, but he's already learned to spell his own name—Dad taught him the four letters he needed to know—and right now, he recognizes three of those.

"It almost spells my name," he says, leaning forward. He looks at his dad. "Why does it say "Tom" twice?"

"Because that's what it's called," his dad says with a shrug. "It's a TomTom."

Tommy frowns, then grins. "Tom-Tom. That sounds funny."

"You like that name?"

"I mean, it's kind of weird."

"Well, suits you then," Dad smiles, reaching over to slap his shoulder playfully. He gestures dramatically with his hand in the air. "And henceforth, he shall be known as Tom-Tom the Curious, and he shall become the conqueror of worlds."

Tommy doesn't quite understand that last part, but it makes him giggle. He says something else to his dad, but the present version of him doesn't pick it up, because the memory is slipping back down into the darkness. The sounds from around him are returning: the sirens, the jeep's engine, the men shouting brief commands at each other, even the girl whimpering.

Tommy blinks and realizes it's only been a split-second. And yet the memory left him with a cutting clarity.

Suddenly, he remembers vividly his dad. His *real* dad. Not the cheap imitation he's been talking to these past weeks.

It feels like he's finally waking up from a lucid dream that he's been caught in for ages. And what's more, he finds that the fear of doing so is not at all overwhelming anymore. In fact, it pops like it was never anything more than a soap bubble.

"This is all wrong," he mutters, barely hearing his own words. "This isn't what I'm meant to do. I got it all upside-down."

Thinking for a brief moment, Tommy adjusts his hold on the machine gun. He swings it slightly to the side, aiming at the back of the nearest gunman.

Then he squeezes the trigger hard. The weapon roars to life and begins spraying bullets.

The girl screams, but her voice is drowned out.

The recoil isn't as hard as he expected, probably thanks to the tripod, but it's still difficult to keep the aim clean, and he can't help but miss with the first half a dozen shots or so. The bullets plow into the jeep, punching holes in the door, the driver's seat, the dashboard. A window shatters, a tire explodes, and the men start shouting in panic and turn around just as Tommy gets the hang of it. Gaining better control of the weapon, he's able to point it at the men and take them down before they realize who's shooting at them. One of them runs around the jeep, ducking for cover, but Tommy catches him in the neck, and he's flung to the pavement. Another fires blindly in the direction of Tommy, getting off three or four shots, which all burrow into the concrete box, before Tommy shoots him in the midsection, causing him to double over with a muffled groan.

It's not at all like in the movies. The men don't spaz out or go flying into the air when he hits them. They simply keel over, clutching whatever part of their body Tommy has hit. Some even stay on their feet for a few seconds, as though not realizing they've been fatally shot. The Vulture starts limp-running away from the jeep, no apparent destination in mind. He's obviously taken at least a handful of bullets, some of them to the right leg, because he's bleeding profusely, leaving a bloody trail. He's also shouting incoherently. It's not even words, more like animal sounds, and it's haunting. After ten steps or so, he slumps to the ground, curls up into a ball, and dies.

Tommy realizes he's no longer firing.

He gets to his feet. His head is ringing. His legs shaking. His hearing all but gone.

Yet his mind is surprisingly calm, even as he looks at the dead men in front of him. Then he looks past the jeep and sees the truck idling right by the end of the trees. Gina is coming out from the pines. It's stupid of her; she's completely exposing herself, and she isn't even aiming her gun anywhere. She's simply standing there, gawking in his direction, taking in the awful scene, and he can tell the exact moment she makes him out, because her expression changes from confusion to one of recognition.

For a moment, they just stare at each other.

"Tommy," she says. At least it looks like that's what she's saying. The siren is deafening, and the sound of the other jeeps are growing louder behind him.

Suddenly, Tommy finds his own voice, and he shouts as loud as he can: "*Go, Gina! This way! Go past me! I'll cover you!*"

Gina hesitates for a second longer. Then she nods once, turns, and sprints back towards the truck.

Tommy spins around to see the next jeep closing in.

He turns the rifle a hundred eighty degrees, lies down, takes aim, and then he begins shooting again.

22

MARK

Holding on to Anton, he drags the boy along with him to the front of the truck.

"What's happening?" John asks as they pass. Lisa is clutching his arm. On the other side is Camilla, holding Danny close. The boy is crying his lungs out—as though he realizes he's back in his mother's arms. Nora is helping her get buckled in.

"Ambush," Mark says, striding towards the window to the cockpit.

"They knew we were coming!" Nora shouts. "I don't know how, but they were ready for us. Fritz almost caught me. Damnit!"

Reaching the window, Mark sticks his arm through and taps Nick's shoulder. "Go! Now!"

Nick looks briefly at him, then points at the side mirror with a grim expression.

"I know. We need to go across the airstrip."

Nick makes a gesture which is quick but unmistakable: He mimics cutting both his wrists.

"I know!" Mark shouts. "I know it's suicide, but there's no other way! Now, *go!*"

Nick gives a single nod, then puts the truck into drive, and they lunge forward. Mark almost loses his balance.

Anton clings to him. "We can't leave my mom!"

"Listen to me!" Mark says, grabbing the boy's upper arm hard, forcing him to look up. "You need to get ready. We might have to leave the truck and make a run for it. If they shoot out the tires—"

He's cut off as an automatic rifle begins blazing nearby. He instinctively ducks and pulls Anton down too, even before John roars out for them to do just that, dragging his daughter to the floor. Nora screams, and Camilla folds herself down over Danny as far as she can go, covering him with her body.

Mark expects to hear and feel projectiles go whizzing by overhead, or—in case the truck really does prove to be bulletproof—at the very least they'll burrow into the side with loud clangs.

But even though the barrage keeps going for several seconds, none of the shots seems to hit the truck.

Either it's a horrible shooter out there, Mark thinks, looking up to see the others squint and gaze around with similar surprise. *Or else ...*

"They're not shooting at us!" John shouts, reading Mark's mind. "I think Gina got hold of a bigger gun. She's covering us!"

No, Mark thinks, not sure where the thought is coming from. *It's not Gina.*

It doesn't really matter. What matters is that they're picking up speed, and so far, the truck has met no resistance. Mark hoists Anton to his feet, then pushes him down into the nearest seat. "Buckle up!" he tells the boy, then goes to Camilla. "Are you both all right?"

Camilla looks up at him, her eyes full of fear, but not panic. "Yes," she says, talking over the sound of Danny crying. "He's OK. They didn't hurt him."

"Thank God," Mark breathes. Then he runs for the back of the truck, almost falling down as Nick turns this way, then the other, as though he's dodging something. They're still accelerating but not as quickly, and Mark can tell from the sound that Nick is only in third gear—probably because he doesn't have a clear path to really gun it yet. Outside, the machine gun is still blazing, and Mark still hasn't heard a single bullet hit the truck. His gun is secured in the holster by his seat, and he grabs it. The truck has two armored windows in the back doors, and he runs to them.

Looking out, the scene is perfectly lit by the sharp floodlights. He's at first confused at what he's seeing.

They've just passed a jeep which is lying upside-down, wheels still spinning. An arm is protruding from the broken driver's side window, and two dead guys are lying on the ground next to the vehicle.

Then they pass the concrete box Mark noticed earlier, and the sound of the gunfire becomes even louder. He sees someone is lying there, almost hidden by shadows, firing a machine gun. From a distance, it's really only the rapid flashes that are visible. Still, they're going by close enough that Mark can make out the shooter.

It's not a man, but a big kid.

It's Tommy.

And he's not shooting at the truck, but at the two jeeps that have now reached the end of the trees and are coming into the airstrip, tires screeching. The first one loses a front tire almost immediately and goes skidding sideways. The other one swerves and dodges the initial hail of bullets. The driver appears to have caught on to where the fire is coming from and tries to go in a wide arch around the concrete box. But Tommy simply follows it with the weapon, only pausing briefly before he starts shooting again. The front window of the jeep shatters, and the driver seems to have been hit, because the vehicle loses speed and comes to a halt, the horn blaring. Out of the doors come three other men, all armed with handguns or assault rifles, and they're immediately mowed down by the bullets still coming at them.

Jesus Christ, Mark thinks to himself. *Glad the kid is back on our side ...*

Then he sees another jeep drive up to the concrete box. It's coming from the opposite direction, and Tommy doesn't appear to have seen it. It stops right next to him.

"Oh, no," Mark whispers, pulling out the binoculars again. "Look out, kid."

But to Mark's surprise, Tommy ceases firing. Instead, he sits up on his knees, gesturing wildly for someone Mark can't see at first. Then a smaller figure—a girl—comes out of the shadow and goes to the jeep. She's walking in an uncertain, hesitant way, and as she comes into the light, Mark recognizes her fiery, red hair.

He sees the door to the jeep open, and Gina steps out. She grabs the girl and all but throws her into the jeep. Then she says something to Tommy, and Mark sees him shake his head.

Gina jumps back into the jeep, and it lunges forward as another jeep comes roaring into view. This one isn't heading for the truck, but for Gina's jeep.

Tommy begins firing again.

That's when Mark turns and shouts: "Anton! Tell Nick to slow down! Your mom is coming!"

23
TOMMY

"Go!" Tommy shouts. "Get out of here!"

"I ... I can't!" Alicia whimpers, stilling cowering in the shadow. "They'll hurt me!"

Tommy whips his head around to hiss at her: "And what do you think Fritz will do if you stay here? He'll think you helped me do this!"

That finally seems to convince the girl. She gets up and steps towards the jeep.

Gina jumps out, grabs her and throws her inside. Then she turns to look at Tommy. "Come with me. Please."

"No," Tommy says firmly. "I said I'm not coming. Just go!"

Gina looks like it pains her to leave him, but she can probably tell from his face that she has no choice—that there's no way in hell Tommy is going with her. She dives in behind the wheel, then guns it, and the jeep shoots off.

Another vehicle is coming, and the guy in the passenger side is hanging out the window, holding a handgun. As he begins firing at Gina's jeep, Tommy wheels the machine gun around and opens fire as well.

It's getting easier already. It only takes him half a second to hit the jeep's front, shatter the windscreen and take out both front tires. The jeep turns abruptly the other way and shoots off towards the tree line.

"I'm getting good at this!" Tommy shouts to no one, his voice breaking.

He turns his head to look after Gina's jeep. He sees it pick up speed, already gaining on the truck. This is partly due to the fact that the truck is slowing down, then stopping completely. Tommy sees Gina come out, dragging Alicia with her, and as the truck's back doors open, Mark reappears to haul them both inside. Then the truck gets moving again. Because of Tommy, it now has a clear run for the south end of the airstrip. The sirens are still blaring, and more jeeps are coming from the hangar, but hopefully Gina and the others will have enough of a head start to—

Tommy senses someone standing behind him. He whips his head around, then gasps.

Fritz has appeared, as though out of thin air. He's staring at Tommy. His eyes are on fire with rage. "What have you done, Tommy?" He gestures to the dead men and the ruined jeeps. "Huh? What did you do?"

The words are barely audible over the wailing sirens. As though Fritz realizes this, his expression turns briefly annoyed, and he makes an almost casual gesture in the direction of the nearest light post, and the siren is killed immediately.

The silence that follows is deafening. Tommy's ears are ringing.

He grabs the machine gun and tries to turn it towards Fritz, but he suddenly can't move it. He realizes it's of course Fritz holding it in place.

"You little turn-coat," Fritz snarls, looking Tommy up and down with disgust. "You helped them get away. We had her trapped, and you—"

"Yeah, I did," Tommy says, letting go of the gun and getting to his feet. "And you know what? Fuck you." He points with his thumb over his shoulder. "You want her so badly? Start jogging, asshole."

Fritz narrows his eyes and lowers his voice to a whisper. "How dare you? I saved you from your pain, and this is how you repay me?"

"You didn't save me from *shit!*" Tommy spits. "You don't take away pain; you cause it! You're a *false* prophet!" He can't believe he's saying this, but at the same time, he realizes there's no turning back. Fritz caught him red-handed, and there's no way in hell Tommy is getting out of this alive, so he may as well speak the truth. He points in the direction of the hangar without taking his eyes off of Fritz. "That thing you created, it's a fucking monster, you know that, right? If you think you can control it, then you're even dumber than I thought. It's going to kill you, man. It's going to kill all of us."

Fritz tilts his head. "You got that partly right." He glances briefly at something over Tommy's shoulder.

Tommy wants to turn around, but he finds himself unable to. Whether it's Fritz holding him, or he's simply paralyzed, he can't tell. A large shadow swallows him up. A puff of warm breath hits the back of his head, and he can smell fresh blood.

Then comes the pain.

24

ANTON

Anton unbuckles and gets to his feet. The truck is swaying and still picking up speed. The engine is roaring, the baby is crying, and outside, the machine gun is firing again.

Anton goes to the window and stands on his toes in order to reach Nick. The guy immediately turns his head to look at him.

"Stop!" Anton mouths. "We need to pick up my mom!"

Nick checks the mirror, then takes his foot off the gas.

Anton looks back through the truck. Nora and Camilla are sitting close together, trying to comfort Danny. John has helped Lisa back up into her seat, and he turns to shout: "What's going on, Mark? I hear a jeep coming!"

"It's Gina!" Mark shouts. "She made it! Tommy's the one firing the machine gun. He's covering for us!"

Anton feels his heart beat even faster. He was sure he wouldn't see his mother again—the thought losing her right after losing Vic was almost too much to bear—and he can't help but run to Mark. He needs to see her with his own eyes.

As Nick stops the truck completely, Anton trips. Mark sees him at the last second and catches him.

"Damnit," he groans. "No running in the aisle."

"Mom!" Anton shouts, staring out of the open door. "Mom, come on! Hurry!"

She doesn't need the instruction; she's already jumped out of still-moving jeep, then yanking out a red-haired girl even younger than Anton. They run to the truck. Gina lifts up the girl, and Mark catches her. Then Gina jumps up, stumbles inside, and Anton throws himself in her arms, almost causing them both to topple over.

"Thank you, thank you," Anton hears himself breathe into her bosom, not really sure who or what he's thanking.

"It's OK, sweetie," his mom pants, stroking his hair once. "I'm here. We're going." That last thing she seems to say to Mark, and he immediately runs to the front to tell Nick. It seems redundant, though, as the truck is already speeding up again. Nick must have followed along in the mirrors.

Anton keeps hugging his mom until she breaks the embrace. "We should sit down," she tells him.

"Everyone OK?" John asks.

Nods and mumbled "yesses."

"I can't believe it," Anton says, almost snorting with laughter. "We did it. We really did it. We got him back, and without anyone getting hurt or killed."

"We're not safe yet," Gina says.

Anton follows her gaze. She has turned to close the door, when something out there seems to have caught her eye.

Anton sees three jeeps that have taken up pursuit. But they're at least two hundred yards away, and they don't seem to be gaining on the truck—as far as Anton can tell, it's a stalemate. In fact, the truck is still picking up a little speed, and they seem to be outrunning the jeeps ever so slightly.

"They can't catch up," Mark says, suddenly standing behind them. "Even if they follow us onto the highway, as long as we can keep driving, it'll be a question of who runs out of gas first. And we made sure the truck had a full tank before we came, so …"

"It's not them," Gina says, not taking her eyes away.

Mark and Anton exchange a brief look.

Anton looks out the open door again.

And then he sees it.

That's the only fitting pronoun—"it." Because while it looks somewhat like an overgrown teenage boy, that's obviously not the case. For one thing, it's way too tall, and its arms and legs are too long. But the way it moves is what really ruins the fragile illusion.

It's coming around the Jeeps, easily outrunning them. It's sprinting on all fours, using both hands and feet, but not like four-legged animals usually do, with the hind legs curling up under the body, propelling it forward. Instead, this creature runs with both arms and legs out to the sides. Anton has never seen anything run like this. The closest association his mind is able to come up with is that of a hunting spider.

Except much bigger. And much faster.

"It'll get us," Anton realizes with a sinking feeling. "It's way too fast."

The truck is going at what must be its maximum speed now.

The creature, however, looks like it's got another couple of gears. Despite how fast it's moving—at least sixty miles an hour now—Anton can tell it's not all-out sprinting. It's able to keep its head surprisingly still, and as it closes in on them, Anton sees how its eyes are too big and too far apart. They're fixed on the truck, and they're ablaze with predatorial hunger. The mouth, which is also too wide, splitting the face like a Muppet doll, is open in what at first looks like a grin, but as it comes closer, Anton can tell it's heaving in air, fueling the superhuman muscles, foam and spittle flying from the thin lips.

For a moment of utter horror, the creature locks eyes with Anton, and they stare at each other. It's only twenty feet away now, and it has matched the speed of the truck.

"Holy fucking hell," Mark says from behind. "Get away from the door, Anton."

He's shoved back as Mark steps up to the door. He pulls out a gun, as does Gina, and they both take aim at the creature.

"As soon as it jumps, start shooting!" his mom shouts.

Anton moves sideways to get a clear view. The creature is even closer now. It lowers its head, and Anton can tell it's about to take off.

Then, at the last second, the monster seems to change its mind.

Anton sees its expression shift, and it slows down. It looks to Anton like someone who received a message through an earpiece. The creature comes to a halt and stands up straight, revealing just how tall it really is. It stands there, its chest pumping in and out, staring after them. But the hunt is over, and they quickly put distance between them.

The truck bumps slightly, and Anton's knees buckle. As he falls to a crouch, he realizes he's shaking and sweating all over.

It could have killed us all. It almost did. But something stopped it.

Anton has no idea what it was. But he's very grateful for it.

25

TOMMY

The pain only lasts for a moment.

Then it's replaced with a rather pleasant feeling. It starts in his chest and flows out into his entire body. The sounds grow distant, silence enveloping the world. The fear leaves him like a group of butterflies taking off, fluttering away, never to be seen again.

Tommy finds himself lying on the ground. He opens his eyes and looks up at the sky.

For the first time in forever, the sky is intact. Unbroken. Perfect. The backdrop is black as ink, thousands of stars glitter, and there's not a cloud to be seen.

Tommy smiles. *I forgot how beautiful it is.*

He feels like staying here. The asphalt isn't even cold. It feels more like a soft bed.

But there's something nudging him. A feeling that he needs to get going.

Am I dead?

Tommy lifts his head and looks down over his body. He expects to see blood and guts, to find his flesh hanging in shreds. But he looks perfectly fine.

Huh. Could have sworn that thing got me.

His clothes have magically been replaced. He's no longer wearing the black shirt and pants. Instead, he's dressed in his regular outfit. Jeans. Sneakers. His favorite T-shirt, the one with that reads "All This and a Big Dick Too." Charles could never stand it and demanded Tommy put on a sweatshirt when he drove him to school.

The thought of his late stepdad is like something from a previous life. Charles was one of the first people to look up at the sky, back when the crack was barely more than a chip. Tommy was right there in the car with him. He almost got beaten to death. And that wasn't the last time he narrowly avoided dying.

I think this time, it finally happened.

He sits up, surprised at how light his body feels, how easily it moves. He's never felt this good. It's like there's no resistance from the air around him. Like he's in a perfect vacuum.

Looking around, he finds that everyone has left. The truck is gone, and so are the gunmen. There are no signs of Fritz or the monster, either. He's all alone on the tarmac.

"You're not alone, Tom-Tom."

Tommy turns his head at his father's voice. He sees him standing only a few feet away—really standing. Gone are the hospital bed, the respirator, the white gown. Dressed in his own clothes, his dad doesn't look sick at all. In fact, he looks better than ever. His eyes are vividly alive, and he's beaming at Tommy.

"Nice to see you again, son. It feels like forever, doesn't it?"

Tommy smiles back. He can't help it. It's been so long since he smiled out of anything other than spite, defensiveness, or because someone cracked a mean joke—those kinds of smiles that never quite reach the eyes. This smile, however, stretches from ear to ear.

Tommy gets to his feet and throws himself into the arms of his dad. The hug is just like he recalls it from when he was little, except tighter and softer and warmer, and it feels like much more than a physical embrace, it feels like they merge. Tommy gives into the sensation.

"I missed you so badly, Dad," Tommy says. "I'm never letting you go."

"You'll never have to," his dad says.

And those are the last words Tommy ever hears.

Because a moment later, Tommy is no more.

26

MARK

"There," Mark says, lowering the hammer. He wipes sweat from his cheek and steps back from the door. "That oughta do it."

Looking back, he sees John getting to his feet, brushing sand from his hands. He's managed to get the bonfire going, and the others are drawing closer, thankful for the light and the warmth. The beach is mostly dark, sunrise still a few hours away, though the moon provides a bluish hue just strong enough for them to cast pale shadows on the sand. The ocean is calm, tiny waves are rolling in like rhythmical breathing, and a slight, salty breeze is in the air.

There's something else in the air, too. It's just outside of what the human senses are supposed to pick up, but Mark feels it, and he's pretty sure the others do too.

It's a form of tension. Or maybe a subtle static. It's like nature itself knows this will be the place for the final stand. As though the air has been electrified with a low current, ready to dial up at any moment.

Not bad scenery, Mark thinks, glancing out over the beach. The water reflects the moon and the stars on its rippled surface, and the sand is smooth like a blanket. Nick and Anton have carried a log close to the fire, and Camilla sits down on it, cradling Danny. Nora is there, right next to her. She hasn't left Camilla's side since handing over Danny. Rex is slinking around, wagging his tail anxiously. Lisa keeps close to John, and Alicia is sitting by herself, darting nervous looks around. She hasn't said much since they arrived. When Mark asked her how she was doing, she just muttered, "fine." He notices she keeps looking at Camilla and Danny.

Poor girl. She feels awful for what she did.

Mark makes a mental note to talk to the girl as soon as he gets the chance. Make sure she knows they don't blame or hold any ill will against her. But right now, there are more important things to do.

He looks at the door again. The two-by-four running across looks solid enough, and he used all the nails, so he feels pretty confident it'll hold. At least for as long as needed. The tiny, wooden beach house was here, just as Mark hoped, and it's the only one in sight. Meaning, it's probably the only door within miles.

"John?" he asks. "Will you give this a test?"

John comes towards him, holding out his hands. Mark takes him by the sleeve and guides him to the door. He feels his way, finding the two-by-four, then giving it a hard yank. The door gives way a few millimeters, and the wood creaks, but it holds.

"I think it's fine," John says, letting go. "It'll take some force to break it open."

"Good. What about the gas?"

John points around the corner of the cottage. "I put it back there. I think we should wait a bit, though. I built the fire against the breeze, so we shouldn't risk a stray spark coming this way, but better safe than sorry."

Mark nods. "Yeah, we wouldn't want to burn down the doorway before Fritz is here."

"Exactly. As soon as it's time, I'll splash it over the walls. It'll only take a few seconds."

"And I'll throw the torch," Mark says, looking at the bonfire. He can tell John purposely placed several long branches so that the ends are sticking out of the fire.

Lisa comes to join them. She's pulled on her sweater, but she still seems to be freezing. "Are you sure it's safe to just, like, sit around?" she asks. "I mean, they knew we were coming, so they can probably tell where we are. Can't they?"

Mark isn't worried that Fritz's gunmen will show up. The Jeeps only followed them to the end of the tarmac, then stopped and turned back. Since then, they've been driving without meeting any other cars.

"I'm not sure," John says, shaking his head slowly. "I think that was because we came very close to their base. That place was ... I don't know. 'Evil' is the best word I can think of. Now that we're fifty miles away, I think we're good."

"I agree with your dad," Mark tells her. "If Fritz could find us easily, he would have done so a long time ago. And he wouldn't have had to use Tommy."

He regrets mentioning Tommy's name, because Lisa's expression immediately turns painful.

"I can't believe he didn't come with us," she whispers, nodding towards Alicia. "If she gets a second chance, why not him?"

"You're not angry with him anymore?" Mark asks, slightly surprised.

Lisa takes a deep breath. "No. I know he caused my mother to die ..." Her voice starts shaking, and she visibly gets a hold of herself. "But it wasn't really him, right? That's what Gina keeps saying. She's forgiven him for killing Victor, so I guess I should forgive him, too."

John puts an arm around her shoulders. "It's up to you how you feel, honey. No one else."

"No, Dad, I get it," Lisa insists. "I really do. When I heard what Tommy was doing for us ... I mean, he's the reason we got away, right?"

Mark nods. "I think that's probably true, yeah."

"That just goes to show Tommy wasn't evil. I've known it all along, really. He was a nice guy. I was even ..." She seems to regret what she's about to say, and instead clears her throat. "He was very caring. Back before his ghost got hold of him. When he came back to the house, I could tell he was different. His eyes, it was like someone else was in there, too. I should have said something, but I wasn't sure what it meant. Thinking back, it's obvious to me that he wasn't the one responsible for setting off that bomb. But what he did tonight ... that *was* his choice. No one forced or even manipulated him to it. He didn't even do it to save himself, because he didn't want to come ..." Her voice grows thin, and she begins crying softly. "And now he's probably dead, right? I mean, Fritz must have found out what he did."

"Most likely," Mark mutters.

Lisa wipes away a tear. "Tommy gave his life for us. As far as I'm concerned, that's enough to right the wrong. I hold no more anger towards him."

With those words, she walks back to the fire, and to Mark's surprise, she sits down next to Alicia. He can't tell what they're saying, but it looks like Lisa strikes up a conversation. Alicia seems hesitant to talk at first, but then she smiles meekly at Lisa.

"You know, I remember a Chinese proverb," John says. "I haven't thought of it since, I don't know, high school, probably. It popped into my mind just now."

"Yeah?"

"It goes something like, 'To learn what's good, a thousand days are not enough. To learn what's evil, an hour is plenty.'"

Mark feels an involuntary shiver run down his back. "That makes a lot of sense."

"Yeah, I didn't really get it back then. I thought of it as bad guys versus good guys, and how it takes a lot of effort to raise a good citizen, whereas it takes very little to fuck someone up to the point of turning them into criminals."

"That's true too, I guess."

"It is, but there's a deeper meaning to it, I think. It's not just about being law-abiding."

Mark looks at John as he seems to consider his next words.

"I think the Chinese referred to our souls," he goes on. "You know? Whatever this is, it's like the ultimate test of our resolve. Like some divine power finally got tired of us messing about and threw us to the wolves. 'Here, figure it out. Hope you're ready, because you had plenty of time.' But … as scary as those wolves are …" John nods towards the barricaded door. "Whatever will come through here before the night is over … the real stand is the one we've been fighting all along." He taps his chest. "The one on the inside. The one for our souls."

Mark thinks it over. "I get it," he says. "Whatever comes of this—whoever wins—it'll be determined by us."

John is about to answer, when another voice beats him to it: "Exactly."

Mark and John both turn to see Gina standing there.

She shrugs. "We are stronger than any monster. As long as we know that and don't allow our courage to falter, we cannot lose." She gestures towards the fire. "Come. Let's go over it one last time. Then we'll make the call."

27
GINA

"All right," Gina says as she finishes the outline. "That's the plan. Any questions?"

She looks around at the faces gathered around the fire. They exchange silent looks, but no one says anything.

"Let's run over it one more time for the cheap seats in the back," John says. He's the only one standing up, his arms folded over his broad chest. "I want to hear everyone say it out loud. We need to make sure we all understand our roles."

"Good idea," Mark chimes in.

"I take Danny to the truck," Camilla says, nodding towards the place in the dunes where they parked the vehicle. "We'll bring Rex and put him in the back. I'm sorry I can't be here with the rest of you, but Danny can't be left alone."

No one argues the point.

"Lisa?" John asks.

Lisa clears her throat. "Anton, Alicia and I, we all go to the dunes. We picked a place where we can see the cottage, but we won't be visible."

"And what's your job?"

"We'll keep our eyes open in case Fritz sends someone to ambush you."

"That's right. And if this ends badly?"

A moment of silence.

Lisa hesitates before she says in a low voice: "Then we run to the truck, and we drive off with Camilla and Danny."

"Exactly," John says. "And you don't look back. You get one of the guns." He gestures towards the cottage by turning his upper body. "As soon as Gina calls up Fritz, I'll douse the cottage in gasoline. And Mark?"

"I'll get ready with the torch," Mark says, looking at the bonfire. "The moment Fritz comes through, I'm setting the whole thing ablaze. That way, no one will be able to follow him through, and he won't be able to leave again, should he change his mind."

"And then we fight," John ends. "Gina gets the other gun. It'll be the five of us against Fritz. Mark, Gina, Nick, Nora, and myself."

Another, long moment of silence. No one seems to know what to say next.

Anton is the one to break the silence. "You'll be like the Avengers," he mutters. He's drawing in the sand with his fingers, and he seems barely aware that he's talking out loud. "Five heroes, defending the fate of the Earth."

Everyone looks at him. Gina can't help but smile. The boys always loved superheroes. She thought they would have outgrown it by now, but both of them always insisted on going to the movies whenever a new blockbuster came out. The first couple of times, Gina was reluctant to go, but she felt they were too young to go alone, so she suffered through Batman, Spiderman, Ironman, Hulk, and a number of others, until she suddenly found herself pulled into the universes. She hated to admit it, but she ended up looking forward to the next one.

"I like the way you think," Mark says with a smile. "But the Avengers have more than five members, don't they?"

"Not the original lineup," Anton says right away. "Same goes for Justice League. They were only five to begin with."

"Well, I stopped watching around the time of Power Rangers," John admits. "There were five of those guys too, right?"

Lisa snickers. "Those were all teenagers, Dad. You're too old to be a Power Ranger."

"Fine, I'm Captain America, then," John retorts. "He's over a hundred, isn't he? That feels about right."

Brief laughter from the group. Some of the tension leaves the air.

Gina looks around at the others, and she can't help but feel a deep love for all of them. As much as she likes the comparison to the Avengers, none of them are superheroes; in fact, they're all painfully ordinary people. A ragtag bunch of survivors, all come together to fight the dark powers.

"All right," she says again. "If there are no questions, I think we should—"

"I—I have something to say."

It's Alicia speaking up; the only one who hasn't said anything yet.

"Sure, what is it, Alicia?"

The girl looks very uncomfortable as everyone looks at her. "I just ... I just wanted to thank you guys ... for bringing me along." The girl's voice trembles, and she's close to tears.

Mark and Camilla are sitting on each side of Alicia, and they both react instinctively. Camilla puts her arm around her, and Mark squeezes her shoulder.

"You're welcome, sweetheart," Camilla smiles.

"And I," Alicia goes on, wiping away a stray tear, "I just feel like … I should be doing something more." She sounds more determined now. "I don't want to be hiding; I want to help."

"There's not really anything you can do," John tells her in a soft voice. "We have it all—"

"I can help Camilla," Alicia says. "I can go with her and Danny to the truck, and I can keep a lookout."

Gina considers it briefly. "I don't think that's a bad idea."

They all look to Camilla for an answer. She strokes Alicia's cheek tenderly, then says: "I'd like that very much."

Alicia smiles.

"Okay, then," Gina says. "It's all in place. I'll go get the phone and make the call."

As the group breaks up, Gina heads for the truck. Nick parked it a hundred yards down the beach, at a place where there's a slope in the dunes low enough to drive through. It's just out of sight from the cottage.

Walking across the sand, she hears running footsteps. Anton catches up with her.

"I'm proud of you," she tells him, pulling him in for a kiss on the temple. "You're very brave. Vic would have been proud too."

Anton looks like the mentioning of his brother is painful. "I'm very afraid," he admits. "But, I'm doing it anyway. That's what you used to tell us, remember? That we shouldn't be afraid of anything bad happening, we just need to know what to do if it does."

Gina nods. "I did tell you that."

They walk for a few moments.

Then Anton says: "Mom, you're Scarlet Witch."

"I'm what now?"

"I'm sorry, but that's her name. Remember, Elizabeth Olsen's character?"

"Oh, right," she says, smiling. "I can live with that. She's very beautiful."

"Yeah, and it's perfect, because she can change reality by tapping into powers greater than herself. Just like you can."

Gina glances sideways at him. "I'm not really sure I'm changing reality, per se. And it's something we all can do, if we—"

"No, it isn't," Anton says, shaking his head. "I know why you're saying it, and in theory, it might be true, but ... you're special, Mom. Whether you like it or not. You're the only one who Fritz can't bully with his powers."

"We don't know that for sure. Perhaps it was a one-time thing. Perhaps I was just immune because of the strong emotions I was feeling after just having lost Vic."

"Well, are those emotions gone?"

Gina sends him another look. "I don't think they ever will be."

"Exactly. That's the power you're tapping into."

Gina considers it. "Well, then I can't be the only one. The power of love isn't exclusive to me."

Anton shrugs. "I guess there could be others like you," he concedes. "I hope so. But not around here. To us, you're special."

"Well, you're special to me," she tells him with a smile.

Anton smiles back. "Now you're just being cheesy, Mom."

She laughs. They've reached the truck, and Gina stops. "Listen, Anton. I want you to be very careful and alert. As soon as you and Lisa go to the hideout, you need to keep your eyes and ears open, okay?"

"Sure, Mom."

She looks out of over the dark beach and the black ocean. "It's becoming desperate. I have felt it ever since Victor died. At the airbase, it was almost palpable in the air. I think this thing we're up against, it knows we have a real chance of winning, and it doesn't like that one bit. So I think it'll throw in everything it's got left."

She can hear Anton swallow. "I'll be ready, Mom."

She looks at him, then pulls him into a tight hug. "You are brave, Anton. Remember that. Whatever happens." She breaks the embrace and kisses his forehead. "Now, go."

He nods once, then turns and jogs away.

Gina stands there for a moment, following him with her eyes until he disappears behind a dune.

She really hopes she'll survive the night. That Anton won't become an orphan. He's already lost his brother, and the thought of leaving him alone in this world is almost too much to bear.

"You're special, Mom. Whether you like it or not."

His words echo in her mind. And she feels the power. It's there, right inside her. Glowing. Emanating from her solar plexus. The love she holds for both her boys.

I am ready, she thinks, taking a deep breath. *Come what may. I am ready to face it.*

28
FRITZ

The voices have left him. For good this time. There's no longer any trace of doubt in his mind.

They're done with him. He knew it would come to this; he just thought it wouldn't come so soon. He was sure he would have a role to play in the final job. The destruction of the resistance. The killing of Gina.

He had his chance, of course. And he let her slip away.

So now, his masters have pulled out, abandoned him as their mouthpiece.

He can feel his powers slipping. Soon, they'll be gone for good. He'll be left exactly as he was before the voices revealed themselves and their true plans for him. It is a cruel destiny. But one he was always aware of. As special as he might have felt, as important a role he had fulfilled, he is still only human, and thus nothing more than a vessel. A thing that served a temporary purpose, only to be cast aside when no longer useful.

Fritz sighs, sinking deeper into the armchair. He feels like he's thirty years older than when this all began.

"It's three o'clock," Frej says from the other end of the lounge, pulling Fritz from his thoughts. He looks across the room to see his son standing by the pool table. The balls are all lined up in front of him, and he's staring at them intently. Picking up one, he squeezes it in his hand, until it breaks with a dry crunch. He lets the pieces drizzle onto the canvas, then picks up another one. "It's three, and she still hasn't called."

Fritz looks at the phone in his lap. The display says 3:01. "I'm sure she will," he says, clearing his throat.

He found the phone inside the package left for him in the building where they kept the baby. It was clearly marked with his name. For a moment, he considered if it might be a bomb. But for one thing, it was too small. It was also wrapped in soft plastic. So, he opened it. Inside was the phone and a brief, handwritten note: GINA WILL CALL AT THREE.

It had made Fritz furious. They had planned out this whole operation, and they had succeeded because they had inside collaborators. Saboteurs. Traitors.

How long had the Twin and the Junkie and the Bomber been working against their cause? Plotting with Gina? For days? Maybe ever since they arrived.

And there was one more. The girl. The Poppy. One of the gunmen who had survived claimed he saw her get into the jeep with Gina.

"And when she does call?" Frej doesn't look at him. He's busy crushing the pool balls. He's been eating ever since they came back inside. Fritz had a group of men load all the corpses onto a truck and bring it here. Now, there's a huge pile of clothes and bones in the corner. The air smells like raw flesh. Some of the gunmen were still alive, barely conscious. Frej ate them anyway.

Fritz can't help but stare at the dried-up blood at the corners of his son's mouth.

"If you think you can control it, then you're even dumber than I thought."

Tommy's last words come to him unbidden, and he shoves them away. He doesn't need to control Frej. Not much longer. And there's relief in that thought. Because the truth is, Frej scares him. It's clear that he's developed his own will. An urge to go out into the world and fulfill his true purpose, instead of sitting around in a basement with his puny, human father.

Fritz was surprised that Frej even listened to him when he shouted for him at the tarmac. He thought for sure Frej would jump onto the truck. And they would have opened fire on him, sending bullets at him from point-blank. Frej was fast, but even he wasn't bulletproof.

To Fritz's great relief and surprise, his son backed down when he heard Fritz's voice in his mind, begging him to stop. Perhaps because he too sensed it was a bit too risky. Either way, Fritz is pretty certain that was last time Frej would do as he was told.

"When she calls, I'll talk to her," Fritz says calmly. "Find out what she wants."

"You know what she wants. She wants me dead."

"Yes, and I won't let that happen."

Frej scoffs. The sound is very good. Very close to perfect. "You can't protect me anymore, Dad. Even if you could, I don't need protection."

"Maybe so," Fritz concedes. "But we still need to be careful. She's dangerous."

"Not as dangerous as I," Frej says, popping a ball into his mouth. Using his molars, he bites down hard, and the ball is crushed. He spits out the broken pieces. "You should have just let me finish it."

Fritz is about to answer, when the phone rings.

He jolts and jumps to his feet, almost dropping the phone. He looks at the screen. It's a seemingly random number calling.

Frej slips around the pool table, his eyes wide and fixed on Fritz. "Answer it," he says, and it sounds much more like a command than a suggestion.

Fritz answers the call and places the phone to his ear. "Gina?"

"*Yes,*" she says simply. "*We want to meet with you, Fritz.*"

Fritz raises his eyebrows. "Oh, really?"

"*We want to talk. Just you and us.*"

Fritz looks at Frej, who's staring back at him, his eyes alive with hunger. "That can be arranged."

"*We're on a beach,*" she says. "*You have to come to us.*"

"Fair enough."

"*Take down these coordinates. They'll take you right to us.*"

She recites a series of numbers. Fritz was always good at remembering numbers, and he doesn't need to write them down.

"*You need to come alone,*" Gina goes on. "*If anyone other than you steps through the door, we'll be forced to shoot.*"

Fritz squints. "How do I know you won't shoot *me*?"

"*You've got my word on it.*"

Fritz scoffs. "Your word. Please. You'll say anything to get me to—"

"*No,*" Gina says. "*I won't. Come alone, Fritz. Come now.*"

"What if I—" The connection is lost as Gina ends the call. Fritz stares at the phone in disbelief. "The nerve ..."

"Let's get going," Frej says, striding to the door. "Open the portal, Dad."

"Hold on," Fritz says. "Just a moment. We need to think."

"No more thinking," Frej says, anger in his voice now as he whirls around to glare at Fritz. "It's time for killing."

"And that's what they're going to do, too," Fritz says, mustering as much resolve as he can. "Look, Son," he says, lowering his voice. "We're going there. Don't worry. But we need to be smart about it. We can't just rush in. It's obviously a trap. As soon as they see you, they'll open fire or—"

"That won't kill me," Frej says right away, shaking his head. "I'm much faster than them. I'll dodge the bullets and rip them apart before they can get off a second shot."

"Then what if they've planted a bomb right on the other side?" Fritz asks. "Or maybe there's a trapdoor, dropping you into a deep pit? The truth is, we have no idea what they've planned out." Fritz looks him up and down. "You're mighty, Frej. But you're no longer immortal. And it's still my job to make sure you're not harmed."

Frej opens and closes his fists, as though still crushing billiard balls. He's visibly fighting to restrain himself. "Then what do you suggest?" The words are pushed out through clenched jaws.

Fritz considers it briefly. He focuses on the door and closes his eyes. And he finds that he can still open the portal. That's good. As far as he can tell, Gina wasn't lying; the destination really is on a beach, and it appears the door she gave him the coordinates for is the only one nearby.

He opens his eyes again. "Let me go first," he says. "If they really have planned something sinister, it's better they get me than you. All right?"

Frej breathes hard. "So I'm supposed to stand aside and wait? Just like last time?"

"Only until I call to you. If I can't handle them on my own, then you come through."

Frej opens his mouth and lets out a long, trembling sigh. "And I'll get to kill her."

"Absolutely," Fritz whispers. "One way or the other, they all die tonight." He turns to the door. As he reaches for the handle, he gets a strong feeling that this will be the last door he ever opens.

I'm going to die too, he thinks with a sudden, striking clarity. *Everyone except Frej will be dead by dawn.*

Then he opens the door.

29

MARK

"Come alone, Fritz," Gina says. "Come now."

Then she lowers the phone and flings it aside.

Mark sees her from the corner of the cottage where he's standing. Gina is out in front of the cottage, flanked by Nick on one side and Nora on the other.

"Go, John!" Gina calls out.

She didn't need to; from the other side of the cottage, Mark can already hear John splashing away with the gasoline. He comes around to Mark's side, pouring the last few drops on the wooden wall, then dropping the can. "Ready," he says, walking briskly past Mark, headed for Gina and the others. Mark is impressed at how well he's navigating without his sight. It's almost become second nature to him already.

Mark looks at the torch in his hand. It should be good for several minutes. But he still hopes Fritz doesn't linger.

The wait is strained. It lasts for what feels like an hour. Probably it's no more than three or four minutes. The electric tension in the air grows stronger, almost like the prelude to a violent thunderstorm. Mark is standing with his weight on one leg, leaning sideways in order to see the door.

Then the handle moves, and the door opens. It swings towards Mark—which is on purpose, as it cuts him from Fritz's view. It also means Mark can't see Fritz. But the cottage is raised half a foot above ground, and Mark sees a pair of black boots step out onto the sand.

"Hello, Fritz," Gina says. "Glad you came."

That last phrase is the cue. Mark backs away another couple of steps. Throwing the burning stick at the wall, it ignites with a deep WHOOP! Some of the gas has evaporated, but there's still more than enough to set the cottage on fire. Bluish flames dart across the wall, engulfing the whole thing in a matter of seconds.

"What the hell …?" he hears Fritz exclaim, as he stumbles away from the door and comes into Mark's view. He covers his face with his hand, shielding it against the light and the heat. He stares at the burning cottage for a moment, then turns back to look at Gina. "A bit dramatic, don't you think? Oh, hi, Mark."

Fritz notices him as Mark walks out to take position, closing the half-circle around Fritz.

"It's been a long time," Mark says. "How's fatherhood treating you? You look a little worn, to tell you the truth."

"I feel better than ever," Fritz says, his voice full of false bravado, and he straightens his back.

"Good, that's good," Mark says. "Can't wait to meet your son. I know you already met mine."

A nerve twitches at the corner of Fritz's mouth. "I hope you know that wasn't personal."

"Funny, it felt very personal," Mark says. He's talking calmly, but on the inside, his emotions are in uproar. Seeing Fritz evokes a lot more anger than he expected. He's also anxious about what's to come. "I trust in return you won't take it personal when I kill your son, then."

Fritz shows his teeth in a sneer. The flames are growing bigger, catching onto the roof. They cast a wavering glow over Fritz's face as he looks at Mark. "You've got it wrong, Mark. My son isn't the one about to die."

"That was the only door for miles," Gina informs Fritz. "You have nowhere to go. This ends here and now, Fritz."

Fritz throws out his arms. "What exactly are you referring to? I'm sure you know our cause is much bigger than me and the people back at the airbase. We are all over the world. New saviors are being born every day. I'm sure by now there are several hundreds. Killing me, it won't do anything."

"We don't want to kill you, Fritz," Gina tells him. "We are giving you a choice. You either help us kill that thing, or we can't let you go back there."

Fritz breaks into a shrill laughter. "That's not really a choice. That's an ultimatum."

"Call it what you like. What's it going to be?"

Fritz squints, looking around at them. "You know my answer. You know I wouldn't betray my own son for anything." His gaze ends on Gina. "Not even under threat."

"I'm sorry to hear that," Gina says, sounding sincere.

"Fritz," Mark says. "Listen to me. This doesn't need to end in bloodshed. Remember how I saved your ass when the blind people tried to kill you?"

Fritz sends him a sour look. "I don't owe you anything."

"I'm not saying you do. But someone else does. Whatever forces are behind this, whatever's been communicating with you … did they explain why the blind people attacked you?"

"Mark, please. Don't embarrass yourself."

"We're not going to change his mind," John says. "It's way too late for that. Believe me on this. I've interviewed enough sociopaths to know when someone is within reach, and when the only thing left is to lock them up and pump them full of drugs."

Those last words seem to trigger something in Fritz. Mark can tell how his posture changes, and his facial expression too. He suddenly looks like he's fighting back a furious anger. "Funny you should phrase it like that," he says, obviously fighting to keep his voice calm. "Because that's just what they did to me. For years I was kept in—"

"Good," John cuts him off. "Should have thrown away the key too. That way you'd still be where you belong."

It's only now Mark realizes that John is talking like this on purpose. He's trying to get Fritz riled up. To make him lose his cool.

"You can keep talking if you want," Fritz says, pointing from John to the rest of them this a thin finger. "But you're already dead. All of you."

"Was it Mommy who didn't love you enough?" John asks, keeping his tone casual, conversational. "Or did Daddy touch your peepee at night?"

Fritz grinds his teeth. "You better—"

"Nah, you were probably born this way. You were insane from the moment you came out of—"

"*I am not insane!*" Fritz screams, causing spit to fly from his mouth. "*I am not sick, and I never was! It's **you**! It was always **you**! **You** are the disease! All of you!*" Fritz heaves in a deep, trembling breath, then lets it out with something akin to laugher. "And now, you all die," he says, his voice dropping.

Fritz stretches out his arms, turns his palms out, and then he makes a series of rapid pushing gestures in the air, aiming at them one at a time. With every push, someone is knocked off their feet. John is first to go, then Nora and Nick. Mark sees it coming and lunges forward, intending to knock out Fritz with a running punch. But he only manages three steps before Fritz pushes in his direction, and something invisible and awfully strong connects with Mark. It feels like a truck. He goes flying backwards.

And then he loses consciousness.

30
ANTON

"Gosh, I really need to pee." Lisa gets up and looks around in the dark, hilly landscape. She points. "I'm just going behind that hill."

"Sure," Anton says. He's sitting on a big stone, ripping a strand of reed into small pieces. He's looking down at the cottage. From up here, his mom and the others look like tiny toy soldiers. The bonfire has almost burned out, reduced to glowing embers. He checks his watch: 2:58. She'll make the call any minute now.

Anton's mind is weirdly empty of thought. It's like the calm before the storm. He knows something crazy is about to go down, but his thoughts have nothing to say about it.

Lisa comes trudging back.

"Did you go already?" Anton asks, not looking at her.

As she doesn't answer, he glances over his shoulder, and he realizes with a startle that it's not Lisa standing there.

It's Victor.

Anton immediately looks away.

Seeing his ghost appear like this, out of nowhere, is a shock to his system.

But, surprisingly, he finds that he was ready for it. In fact, this was the storm his mind was waiting for.

This is it. I need to be brave.

Even as he tells himself this, he feels the fear wash through him, his heart rate rising and his palms growing sweaty.

"Look at me, Ant," Victor says, his voice playful. "Look at me! Or are you too chickenshit to look at your own brother?"

Anton turns his head and looks at Victor. Doing so requires a lot of effort, even though he tries to act casual.

His brother is grinning in that special way that's so unique to him. He's done it ever since they were very little. The grin always meant Victor was up to something mean. But Anton can tell it's a clever imitation. He grew up right alongside Victor. He has seen him every day, has never spent more than a few hours away from him. He can easily tell a pretender from the real deal. And for some reason, that immediately diminishes his fear.

"I'm not afraid to look at you," Anton hears himself say. "Because you're not my brother."

Victor's grin falters, but only a little. "You don't mean that. You're terrified. I can feel it. Your heart is pounding away."

Anton shrugs. "Of course it is. And of course I am. Scared, I mean. But not of you. You're not real."

Victor shows his teeth in a sneer. "Cut the crap, Ant. First you let me die, and then you—"

Anton snorts. The noise escapes him before he can help it.

Victor glares at him. "What? You're saying you didn't cause my death? If you'd stopped me from running to help Patrick, then I would still be alive."

Anton grimaces. Not because of what the ghost is saying, but because of the memory it evokes.

Victor. His brother. Dead.

It's very painful. But it also serves to make him believe what he's seeing even less.

"Listen," he says. "Victor was my twin brother. I knew him better than I know myself. I loved him more than I love myself. And there's no way in hell you're going to convince me that wasn't how he felt too, because I know it is." He looks the ghost up and down, shaking his head. "You're not even doing a good job impersonating him. Mom said you were getting desperate, and I guess she was right. She said—"

"Mom," Victor sneers. "That stupid bitch. What did she ever do—"

"Shut up and listen," Anton says. The ghost blinks with surprise, and Anton goes on before it can say anything else. "I knew you would choose Victor to try and fool me. I knew it the moment he died. And I knew that whatever bullcrap you'd have him tell me, I wouldn't believe it for a second. In order to be afraid of something, you need to believe it. So, if you don't mind …" Anton stretches his neck, and blows a thin stream of breath into the face of the thing in front of him. "Go away, Ghosty. I'm done talking to you."

He turns his head away. Then he does his best not to move or look back. Out the corner of his eye, he can see the imitation of his brother still standing there. Can hear it breathing fast. It's angry. Furious. No doubt looking for a new angle to work him.

Then, suddenly, it starts growing. It gets bigger and bigger, until it looms over Anton. Still, he doesn't look at it. He breathes firmly through his nose, repeating the mantra in his mind, over and over again.

I am brave. I am brave.

The ghost leans over him and opens its mouth, letting out a loud, drawn-out wail. Anton feels its icy breath blow against his hair, and the thing screams louder and louder until he's sure his eardrums will burst, and he's very close to moving out of the way, but instead he starts shouting the mantra in his thoughts, and—

Then it's over.

The ghost disappears with a sigh.

Anton blinks and looks around. His heart is still thumping away in his chest, but his body feels very different. Lighter. Less scared.

He sees Lisa come around the hill. She's staring at him with big, white eyes.

"What is it?" he whispers. "You look like you just saw a ghost too."

"I did," Lisa says, sounding almost like someone under hypnosis. She breaks into a smile. "And I let go of her. Completely. She went away."

Anton gets to his feet. "Great job."

Lisa tilts her head. "You said 'too' ... Did you also ...?"

"I did," he says. "And I made it go away too."

Lisa grabs him and pulls him into a tight hug. Anton hugs her back.

As they let go, Anton looks at his watch again. "Jeez, it's 3:11. How could so much time have passed?"

They both turn to look down at the cottage.

What they see is terrifying.

"Oh, no," Lisa breathes. "They're losing. We need to go, Ant."

"Wait, just wait," Anton says.

"We promised we would go," Lisa says. "For Camilla and Danny's sake!"

Anton can't take his eyes off the fighting going on down there. "You're right," he hears himself say. "You go. Get them to safety. I'm staying."

Lisa says something else. She pleads with him. Tries to pull him along.

But Anton isn't budging.

He just keeps staring.

31
GINA

As Fritz throws out his arms, Gina knows something is about to happen. But she doesn't know what, so she only pulls back a little, not going for her gun.

One at a time, Fritz knocks them all back. Mark is the last one to go, and he almost manages to reach Fritz. Almost.

Finally, it's only Gina standing. The others are rolling around in the sand, groaning and panting, obviously hurt from the invisible force that hit them.

Fritz glares at Gina. He's breathing fast and grinding his teeth. "I always knew I was going to kill you, Gina. I just didn't imagine I would have to do it myself."

"Well," Gina says, showing her hands empty. "Here's your chance."

Fritz balls both his hands into fists, squeezes them against his chest, and then he thrusts them towards Gina with a grunt of exertion.

Gina doesn't feel a thing. She begins walking towards Fritz. His expression turns from triumph to disbelief. "No. Not again. What's wrong?" He repeats the thrust three times, putting more and more effort into it, but to no avail.

Gina stops just outside of his reach. "Whatever black magic you're using, it doesn't seem to work on me."

"I don't ... I don't understand," Fritz barks, shaking his hands, then tries yet again to blast Gina away.

"Kick his ass, Gina," John croaks from somewhere nearby.

Fritz takes his eyes from Gina a split-second, looking in the direction of John. Then he stares back at Gina, his lips quivering, and he takes a wild swing at Gina's head. She sees it coming and easily ducks below it. She counters with a foot-stomp and a knee to the gut. Fritz cries out in pain and doubles over. His scream turns into a roar of rage as he charges her like a bull. Gina steps out of the way, sweeps his legs and elbows him hard in the back. He falls to the ground with another hoarse cry. In one last desperate attempt, he grabs her ankle, wanting to pull her leg out from under her. Gina simply steps on his wrist with her other shoe, and Fritz wails.

"Ow! Get off! Get off, you'll break it!"

Gina lifts her foot, and Fritz immediately scrambles to his feet, clutching his wrist. He doesn't look like he wants to fight anymore. He looks around like a cornered animal. With the exception of Mark, who's been knocked out, the others have gotten to their feet and reformed the half-circle. Their faces are lit by the flickering light from the roaring flames. Even from this distance, Gina can feel the heat.

"I knew your powers didn't work on me," Gina tells Fritz, pulling out the gun. "That's why I have the weapon."

Fritz glares from the gun in her hand to her eyes, still rubbing his wrist and breathing hard. They have switched places now, so that Gina is standing with her back towards the burning cottage. Maybe that's why she sees Fritz's eyes shift.

"Funny you should mention it," he whispers, running his tongue across his lips. "I've got a weapon too."

Gina halfway expects him to pull out a gun—and she's ready to fire if he does.

But instead, he looks past her, forms a funnel around his mouth with his hands, and bellows: "*Frej! Could you join us, please?*"

32

NICK

For a moment, nothing happens.

They all just stare at the burning cottage. The doorway is almost gone now, having been swallowed up by the flames.

Then, emerging out of the fire, steps the most horrid thing Nick has ever seen.

It's much bigger than he thought.

It's also on fire.

As it steps out onto the sand, its clothes are all ablaze. It doesn't seem at all bothered by it, though. Smoldering fabric drizzling from its huge frame, it brushes off the last of the embers, revealing large, red burn wounds all over. It turns its thin neck to look around at them in turn, smiling as it begins to speak with a voice that Nick is glad he can't hear. It must be very deep, because he feels it in his bones as he reads the words from its unnaturally wide mouth.

"I know no pain. I know no fear. I cannot die."

Even as the creature speaks, the patches of burned skin are closing up, disappearing without scars. What he sees makes Nick doubt—really doubt—that they can kill this thing. If it can regenerate bodily trauma almost instantly, what will they have to do to kill it?

"This world is mine now," the creature goes on. "And you are no longer welcome in it."

Fritz gets to his feet and slips around Gina. Approaching the monster, he reaches up a hand, apparently wanting to place it on the creature's shoulder. He's saying something, but because of the angle, Nick only catches the last part: "... proud of you, Son."

Then, not even looking at him, the creature strikes Fritz in the side like someone swatting at an irritating fly. The slap—while seemingly not intended to hurt—is still strong enough to send Fritz flying sideways, landing on the sand and rolling around like a ragdoll. He stops in front of Nora, and she instinctively jumps aside.

Fritz sits up, his face a mask of shock and horror, and then he doubles over in pain, clutching his side. He visibly fights to draw in breath, as he turns and crawls away awkwardly, only using one hand.

"I will kill you all now," the creature says, still just standing there. "I will eat off of your flesh and break your bones and rip off your skin while you're still alive. There will be pain like you've never felt before. That is the punishment you get for challenging me. You will—"

What happens next plays out so fast, Nick barely has time to take it all in.

John moves first. He suddenly charges right at the creature, like a quarterback about to tackle another player. For a guy his size, he crosses the distance incredibly fast.

At the same time, Nora cries out and flings a rock the size of an apple right at the back of the creature—who has already turned to face John. The stone connects right between the shoulder blades, and the creature's attention is drawn away from John for just a split-second. That's when John jumps and throws himself into the side of the creature, connecting with his good shoulder.

While the monster is very thin and appears like it should be easy to take down, it looks more like John runs into a tree. He does manage to push the creature back a few steps as it regains its bearings, and he immediately grabs it in what looks like some kind of jiu-jitsu hold, catching its arm and pulling it down, then pinning it under his own bad arm and twisting it upwards with the other. The hold should be enough to break the creature's elbow, except the joint seems able to bend way more than even the most flexible person would. The monster is still obviously annoyed by it, and it tries to grab John by the throat while tugging to get the other arm free. But John has clamped down with all his body weight, forcing the arm to the sand, causing the creature to bend over.

"*Get it!*" John roars. "*Shoot it, Gina!*"

Nick looks over at Gina. She has aimed the gun at the creature, but is hesitating.

She doesn't want to risk hitting John.

Then Nora comes running from the other side, going for the creature's leg. Nick finds himself moving forward, instinctively wanting to protect his sister.

A moment before she reaches the creature, it manages to grab John around the chest and lifts him clean off the ground. It then roars out and throws him away like a kid tossing a softball. John goes by right over Nick's head, whirling around as he flies into the darkness.

The creature doesn't skip a beat, but turns around and catches Nora by the neck. It lifts her up, opens its giant mouth and is about to bite her face, when Nick reaches it and delivers a running kick to the side of its knee. The creature doesn't drop Nora, but it twists its body around with the speed of snake striking, and before Nick can get out of the way, it bites him instead.

It happens so fast, he barely feels it. It's nothing more than a nip at the neck.

The monster pulls its head back again and chows down what appears to be a large, bloody lump of flesh.

Nick's hand goes to his neck, and it's immediately drenched in the waterfall of blood that's gushing out.

The monster—no longer considering Nick a threat—turns its attention back to Nora, who's still hanging suspended in the air. Her face is turning red, and as her eyes meet Nick's, they look at each other for the last time, and Nick thinks to himself just before he collapses: *I bought you five seconds. Hope that's enough. Love you, Nora.*

Then he collapses and dies.

33

MARK

He's only gone for a few minutes.

It's the sound of gunfire that brings him back.

He sits up, dizzy and confused, a splitting headache banging inside his head. He feels sand under his hands, and he looks up to see a big, roaring fire.

Then it all comes back to him.

In front of the burning cottage is the creature. In its hand is Nora, her feet dangling in the air, her face all red and swollen from being suffocated.

On the ground is Nick, his throat having been ripped out.

John is nowhere in sight. Neither is Fritz.

Gina is the one doing the shooting. She's walking towards the monster, unloading the magazine as she does, and the creature does what looks like a crazy dance. At first, Mark thinks it's being hit by the bullets, and that's why it's moving the way it does. Then he realizes to his dismay that it's in fact dodging the bullets.

But as Gina comes closer, two or three connect—Mark can tell from the screechy shrieks the monster gives off, along with the small sprays of blood coming out the back of the creature. It's finally forced to let go of Nora, and she flops to the sand, heaving for breath as she crawls away.

The creature spins around and throws itself at Gina.

She manages to get out of the way, but not completely. The monster catches her with one hand, knocking the gun away. It then pounces on her, and to Mark, it looks like a grown-up attacking a fourth-grader. The monster swings at her, tries to scratch her, to grab her, to bite her. Gina backs up as she moves deftly to defend herself, using both arms, and she avoids the worst of the onslaught. Then the monster catches her with a crushing blow to the shoulder, and Gina is knocked to the ground.

The monster towers over her, and Mark tries to shout in order to draw its attention, but his voice is gone, so instead he gets to his feet. As he does, he notices the stick he used to set the cottage on fire. One end is still glowing with embers. He grabs it. The pain in his skull intensifies, but he barely feels it. He just staggers towards the monster, who has its back turned.

I won't make it.

But the monster doesn't kill Gina right away, even though it surely could. She's lying on the sand, clutching her shoulder, staring defiantly up at it.

"You never stood a chance, Gina," the creature bleats, its voice full of triumph. "You were always destined to lose. You see, we are a force that can never die. You might think you've got us beaten, but the moment you glance away, we will rise again. We are more than immortal, Gina. We are eternal."

As Mark comes up behind the creature, Gina seems to sense him, but she doesn't look away from the monster's face, not even for a split-second. Instead, she says through gritted teeth: "You might have been immortal when you were hiding behind the curtains. But now you're in our world, and as far as I can tell, you're already bleeding."

The monster bends over, about to grab Gina and rip her apart, when Mark stabs the glowing stick into its side.

The creature roars out, turns around and grabs Mark around the waist. It does so with such terrifying speed, Mark doesn't have time to react. Before he knows it, it has wrapped its long, thin arms around his midsection and lifted him clean off the ground. It feels like being caught in an industrial car crusher. If Mark wasn't already convinced the creature possesses enormous strength, he feels it now, as it begins tightening its grip. He becomes immediately unable to breathe, and he feels his lower ribs bend painfully inwards, threatening to puncture his organs. Both his arms are pinned, so he tries to kick the creature, but at that moment, it gives a violent tug, crushing him even more, and Mark feels something in his spine give way.

He roars out in agony, but surprisingly, the pain fades quickly. Initially, he takes it as a good sign, but then he realizes he can no longer move his legs. In fact, he can't he feel anything from the waist down.

It paralyzed me. Broke my goddamn spine.

The creature, still tightening its death grip, stares at Mark with horrible, perverted glee radiating off its face. It reveals its pointy teeth in a wide smile. They're almost at eye level, Mark sitting slightly higher, and he wriggles desperately to get his arms free, to break the bear hug, to get even a tiny amount of air into his lungs, which by now feel like they're about to burst along with his bowels, liver, kidneys and everything else inside of him.

The creature just keeps staring at him, taking in every little emotion coming off his face, lapping it up, relishing in his anguish.

"Die, Mark," it sneers, barely any strain in its voice. "Leave this world. Perish like a worthless insect. Your son will follow shortly. I know he's nearby. I can smell him."

Those last words ignite something in Mark. He's already running on basal instincts, but the thought of Danny kicks him into all-out primal mode. What's left of his energy turns in a heartbeat into a fiery fury, and he does the only thing he can: He leans back, then flings his head forward, whamming his forehead into the creature's face.

The head-butt is so hard, it makes black spots appear in front of Mark's eyes, and for a split-second, the world spins around itself, and he comes very close to passing out again.

Then, miraculously, air seeps into his lungs, and the pain of them expanding is what snaps him back. He's still caught in the creature's grip, but it has loosened it just enough that Mark can suck in a much-needed breath. He blinks away the last of the dizziness. The creature is still staring at him, but it appears surprised and slightly disoriented. A dark-red bruise is emerging between its eyes.

Still being run by that primal energy, Mark's body seems to act on its own accord. He pries his right arm free, then tries to pull the left one out too, but the creature regains its bearings just in time to close the grip again, pinning it in place.

Mark groans as the creature once again applies enough pressure for him to be unable to breathe. Through his teeth, he wheezes: "Go back ... to being ... blind, asshole."

Forming the sign of the devil, he punches the creature right on the bridge of its nose, and in doing so, plunges his pinky and index finger deep into the eye sockets. He feels one of the eyeballs burst with a wet pop.

This time, the creature roars out—the sound is definitely not human; it sounds more like a raptor—and as it pulls back, it releases the hold on Mark, and he drops to the ground. Landing on his legs, they do nothing to keep him upright, and he flops onto his side with a gasp of pain from his back.

The creature screams loudly, the sound goes into a pitch so high, Mark's ears start to ring. It clutches its bleeding eyes, then lashes out blindly at Mark, hitting nothing but air.

Mark turns over, feeling his bones and intestines cry out as they readjust to their original positions. He has no idea if anything other than his back is broken or ruptured, but at least his arms are working, and he elbows his way forward, away from the creature.

34
CAMILLA

Danny lets go of her nipple and leans back his head with a sigh.

Camilla tucks her breast away before it can spray any leftover milk, and then she dabs his lips. He's already far gone and doesn't notice it.

She looks at him and feels waves of love radiate through her. "I'm never leaving you again, I hope you know that. So you'll have to come to terms with living with your mother for the rest of your life."

Danny grunts in his sleep.

She wraps him in the blanket and gently puts him down on the seat next to her. She is sitting behind the wheel of the truck. It's facing away from the beach, ready to drive out of here if it becomes necessary. She checks the mirrors again, even though she can't see the cottage from here.

"I really hope your father is OK," she whispers, biting her lip.

It feels wrong, sitting here, while the others fight for the fate of the world. But irrational as it may be, her maternal instincts are stronger, and protecting Danny takes priority. She has already almost lost him once, and it's never happening again.

She's still staring into the mirror, when a figure suddenly comes jumping down from the nearest dune and runs towards the truck. She recognizes Alicia, and she rolls down the window.

The girl comes to her door and stares up at her with big eyes full of alarm. "Fritz," she pants. "He's coming."

"Coming *here*?" Camilla asks.

"Uh-huh. I saw him. The monster, it's come through the door, too, and the others are fighting it. But Fritz walked off, and ... and I didn't see him until he was right next to me. He must have taken another path here, and—"

"Get in the truck," Camilla interrupts, twisting the key.

The engine roars to life as Alicia runs around the front. She opens the door and is about to climb into the truck, when Camilla turns on the headlights and almost screams. Right there, twenty feet away, is Fritz. He's visibly hurt, clutching his side, while shielding his eyes with the other.

Alicia gasps and freezes as she sees Fritz.

"Come on," Camilla whispers. "Get in!"

But Alicia is paralyzed.

"Turn off that light," Fritz shouts, waving his hand. And, magically, without Camilla having to touch anything, the headlights die.

Camilla turns her head to look at Alicia, but the girl is gone. "Damnit!" She places one hand on Danny, puts it into drive, and then she floors it.

But Fritz makes another gesture, and the engine dies just as the truck is about to leap forward.

"Fuck!" Camilla scrambles to unbuckle and pick up Danny. When she finally manages to open the door, Fritz is standing there.

There's a look of recognition in his eyes as he sees her. "So you're the getaway driver, huh?"

Camilla's mind is working fast. She needs the gun. It's on the dashboard. Fritz can't see it from where he's standing. But as soon as she goes for it, he'll see it, and he'll take it from her. She needs to surprise him. The problem is, he's staring right at her.

"You can take the truck," she says. "Just let us get out."

"Hold on," Fritz says, raising his hand. "I can't let you go."

"Why not?"

"Because I can't drive." He winces, then mutters: "He broke my damn ribs ... ungrateful bastard." He looks back up at her. "Kids, huh? You do everything to protect them, and then they suddenly lash out at you. And yet you still love them."

What Fritz is saying is so grotesque, Camilla is struck by a feeling of unreality. It's like they're old acquaintances who've bumped into each other at the grocery store.

"Please, Fritz. Let me go. For Danny's sake. He's been through enough."

Fritz looks at the bundle in her arms and seems to consider it for a second. Then he shakes his head. "I told you, I can't drive. You'll have to do it."

He closes the door and walks around the front of the truck.

Camilla puts Danny back down onto the seat, grabs the gun, and fumbles with the safety. Mark showed her several times how to do it, and she was sure she had the hang of it, but of course it gives her trouble now that it's not a practice situation. As Fritz climbs into the passenger seat, she's still fumbling with it. He hasn't noticed, because he's busy with his hurting side. He tells her to turn on the engine. "We need to get going."

She finally gets the safety to budge, just as Fritz turns his head to look at her.

He realizes the danger a split-second before she can pull the trigger, and then she can't.

"Holy cow," Fritz exclaims. "I didn't know you had a gun ..."

Camilla strains hard to squeeze the trigger, but it's like it's welded in place. She hisses and tries again. Her arms begin to shake with the effort, but it's no use.

Fritz expression turns dark. "I can't believe you were about to shoot me. I would have let you go, eventually. You and your boy. But now ..." He shakes his head. "You know what? I'm going to teach you a lesson, Camilla."

"No," Camilla says, pointing the gun towards the ceiling. "No, Fritz."

"Yes," he says. "If I'm going to be able to trust you, I need to know you're afraid of me. That I mean what I say." He throws out his hands. "You just tried to shoot me in the face! I have crucified people for much less."

"Fritz, don't do this. Just take the truck."

"I ... can't ... drive," he says, spelling out the words. "Now, let's get it over with." He wiggles a finger, and Camilla feels invisible hands take control of her arm. She lifts the gun and points it down at Danny.

"No!" she cries out, trying desperately to pull her arm away, to aim the gun anywhere else. She can't do it, so she instead covers the muzzle with her other hand. "No, no, no! Fritz, please!" She stares at him in earnest. "I beg you. Kill me instead!"

Rex starts barking from the back.

Fritz glances briefly back, then shrugs. "Who'll drive the truck, then?" The complete lack of emotion in his voice makes Camilla even more terrified than she already is. There's no trace of doubt left in her mind that Fritz will make her kill Danny just to make sure she'll obey him in the future. She tries again to pull away the gun, to get up from the seat, to do anything, but Fritz has her entire body pinned in place. He's in full control over her.

Because of Camilla's shouting, Danny is starting to wake back up. He moves and grunts.

"Now, tell him goodbye," Fritz says, wiggling his finger again.

"Nooo!" Camilla screams, and then she pulls the trigger.

The gun clicks.

Fritz sighs. "You didn't load it? That's OK, let me show you." He controls her hands, and she loads the gun. As he turns her back towards Danny, Camilla sees Alicia. She's standing outside the truck, her head close to Fritz's feet.

Just as Camilla raises the gun again, Alicia opens her mouth and bites down hard on Fritz's ankle.

He yelps and jerks and spins around to see what caused the sudden pain.

And Camilla at once regains control over her body.

"You!" Fritz roars out. "You little piece of—" Then, apparently recalling that Camilla has a gun, he turns back around. As he does so, Camilla shoots him twice in the chest.

Fritz looks shocked for a moment. Then he doubles over, almost lying down on top of Danny. Camilla drops the gun and catches him, pushing him away hard. With a groan, Fritz tilts backwards and topples out of the truck.

"Alicia?" Camilla calls out, picking up Danny, who's screaming now. She can barely hear it. "Alicia, sweetie? Are you OK?"

For a terrifying moment, she's afraid that she might have shot Alicia too. She was standing right behind Fritz, and even though the angle was wrong, a bullet could have gone astray, and—

And then Alicia appears in the door. She looks first at Fritz, then up at Camilla.

"Oh, my God," Camilla breathes, rocking Danny, releasing the immense shock of almost being forced to shoot her own son. "It's all right, baby. Calm down. Mommy's here."

"Is he OK?" Alicia asks, looking at Danny. "Is he hurt?"

"No, he's just crying because of the gun going off."

"Good," Alicia nods, looking one last time down at Fritz. He's stopped moving and makes no sounds.

"Thank you," Camilla says. "Thank you, thank you, Alicia."

The girl looks back up at her, sending her a pale smile. "Don't mention it. I owed him."

35
GINA

As soon as the monster turns towards Mark, Gina goes for the gun.

It's the only way to kill it.

She crawls this way then that, squinting her eyes to see. The gun is nowhere in sight, but it must be close by. She keeps crawling farther and farther away from the light, searching the sand frantically.

Behind her, she can hear Mark give off a groan of pain, and the creature begins talking to him. She glances back briefly, seeing it hold Mark in a bear hug. Her instincts scream at her to run back and help him, but she knows that it'll be futile. Without the gun, they're both dead, just like Nick.

"Gina ..."

A weak voice from the darkness somewhere.

"John?"

"Here," he says. "I felt it. It landed right next to me. Take it."

Gina crawls quickly in the direction of his voice. She finds him lying on his back, holding up the sand-covered gun. He looks beaten up, but he's not bleeding. At least not outwardly.

"Kill it," he hisses. "Hurry."

Gina rips the gun from his hand and gets to her feet. Her right shoulder is throbbing; if she survives the night, her arm will be useless tomorrow. Right now, however, she's fueled by adrenaline, and her arm is able to raise the gun as she runs towards the monster.

She has no idea how many bullets she fired already, but she knows there can't be many left. Three if she's lucky. So she needs to make them count. Anything less than a headshot or a bullet right to the heart region is unlikely to stop the creature.

To her surprise, the monster has dropped Mark—and he's still alive. It doesn't seem interested in picking him back up; in fact, it staggers away from him, clutching its face.

What did he do to it?

As the creature turns towards her—more out of pure luck than because it senses her coming—it takes its hands away and blinks its eyes open. They're both bleeding, and one eyeball appears to have been punctured. The other must still be working, because it focuses on Gina, and the creature's face morphs into a mask of utter rage.

With an inarticulate cry it lunges at her. Gina fires the gun twice. One of the shots burrow into the monster's collarbone. The other takes off a piece of its ear. None of them stops it.

It reaches her in a heartbeat, and then it bites.

It happens faster than a blink of an eye.

One moment, the gun is there. The next, it's gone. And so is her hand.

Gina stares at the bones of her forearm protruding from the bloody stump of her wrist as the blood begins pumping out. The creature turns its head sideways and spits out the gun along with her severed hand. Then it lunges at Gina again, knocks her to the ground and lands on top of her.

Using both arms, she forms a cross right in front of her face, only just managing to catch the creature under the jaw as it snaps its teeth inches from her nose. Pressing down on her, Gina can tell it's way heavier and way stronger than it looks, and she can't hold it. Her own, warm blood, spilling from the place where her right hand sat just seconds ago, is splashing all over her neck and face, and she turns her head sideways to avoid getting it in her eyes and mouth.

Gina does the only thing she can: She kicks the creature hard in the groin. She has no idea if it's got genitals. If it can even be considered a male.

But based on its reaction, she clearly hits something tender, because the creature gives off a shrill howl and pulls its midsection back a little. Gina kicks again, but this time, the creature is prepared and squeezes its legs together, catching her ankle.

It then leans over her again, its chin still resting on Gina's crossed arms, and it stares at her with wild, bleeding eyes, only the left one still seeing. As its face come closer, Gina stares back up at it, taking in the awful sight, and she realizes this is the last thing she'll see. In a second, the creature will bite off her face or dig into her throat, and she will die.

As the creature opens its giant mouth, revealing the teeth, the pink gums, and farther back, the opening to the soft, slimy throat, Gina closes her eyes and forces time to slow down, not in the physical reality, but in the reality of her mind, and she calls forth her boys, their faces happy and untroubled, their smiles innocent and cheeky, just like they used to look before all this happened, and she takes it all in, every single detail of them, and it fills her with a love and a joy so radiant, everything else goes away, the pain, the fear, the adrenaline coursing through her, and she is ready.

Then it comes.

A voice.

Anton.

At first, Gina is sure she's only hearing him in a memory. But she's never heard him say these exact words before.

"This is for my brother."

Gina opens her eyes again, and reality comes rushing back. Her view is completely blocked by the open mouth of the creature, its warm breath and sticky saliva pouring down over her.

Then, apparently hearing Anton's words, the creature whips its head to the side, and the expression of triumph turns to grim surprise.

Gina sees her boy, her only living son, standing there, silhouetted against the black sky. His face is set in stone, his hand holds the bloody, sand-crusted gun. And it doesn't shake in the least.

"This is for Victor," Anton says.

Then he pulls the trigger.

Gina sees the flash, sees Anton's arm jerk back, and she sees the scarlet volcano erupt from the back of the creature's skull as it's flung to the ground, the pressure of it easing from her chest.

Then the sound follows, slamming against her eardrums, reducing her hearing to a low buzz, not unlike the ocean.

Gina takes one last, deep breath, lets it back out, and then she's gone.

36
GINA

As she watches the streets glide by outside the bus window, Gina's mind keeps going back to what she just went through.

She keeps hearing the sound of the skater's collarbone breaking as he hit the ground. Keeps feeling the woman's hands around her neck, unnaturally strong, squeezing the life out of her.

But mostly what haunts her is the young girl with her backpack.

That could have so easily been one of my boys.

The mere thought of Victor or Anton getting struck blind and insane is enough for Gina to shiver and give off an involuntary sound.

The girl on the seat across from her looks over at her. "I know, it's insane, right?"

She nods towards the screen suspended from the ceiling. It's showing scenes from downtown. Police cars and ambulances are everywhere, debris and body bags littering the streets. The headline reads: *Chaos and mass killings in three cities*!

"They still don't know what caused it," the girl goes on. "At least they're not saying."

"I do," Gina says. "I know what caused it."

Something strange happens in her mind as she speaks the words. It's like a movie, skipping a few frames.

The girl looks at her, cocking her head. "You do? What is it?"

"It's these ... evil entities. They're of us, really. Our darkest, innermost fear and hatred."

The girl raises her eyebrow in an exaggerated look of surprise. "Wow, uhm, all right, then. If you say so." Her phone rings and she answers it immediately. "Mom? Yeah, I'm on my way. No no, I'm fine."

That was weird, Gina thinks. *She thought I was crazy.*

She blinks and looks out the window again. This part of town looks completely normal. Cars parked neatly at the side of the road. Pedestrians walking. Windows intact. It's a jarring contrast to the scenes on television.

Gina still can't believe she lied to the authorities. But she just couldn't risk getting stuck in that room for hours on end. She'd seen enough crime shows to know what it meant when you were taken to a small room with two officers dressed in suits seated across from you.

She had to go get her boys. They were her priority. Always had been, always would be. Apparently, even national security came second to that.

Gina closes her eyes briefly, and the skipping feeling comes again, stronger this time.

She opens her eyes again, and finds herself standing outside the bus. As soon as it drives off, Gina crosses the street and jogs into the schoolyard. And there she sees them, sitting on the stairs by the main entrance. Anton is playing on his phone while Victor is busy balancing a stick on the back of his hand.

Gina's heart leaps with relief as she runs to them. "God, am I glad to see you guys!"

She bends over to cover their cheeks with kisses—something they hate her for doing in public. Right now, she couldn't care less. And probably because of the situation, they don't offer any protests.

"You all right, Mom?" Anton asks, putting his phone away. "They told us Frederik's dad was working down there when it happened and they don't know if he's OK."

"Yes, and Lisa from seventh grade, her grandma died!"

"I'm fine, nothing happened to me," Gina assures them. "The police came and helped me."

"But the police can't really help us," Victor asks. "Can they?"

Gina looks at him, thinking: *That's not what he said. He asked me something else.*

"I mean, you said so yourself," Victor goes on. "It's up to us to stop this."

"All right, listen," Gina says, stopping. She pulls the boys in front of her to look at them—she hardly needs to bend her knees for them to be at eye level, so much have they grown this past year. "What happened," she says, then correcting herself. "What *is going to* happen … it'll change the world forever. It'll change *us.*"

"But, Mom—"

"Let me finish. It will tear us apart, and then it'll bring us closer together, and then … then tear us apart again. Forever." Those last words come out as barely more than a whisper, as Gina suddenly realizes what she's saying. Somehow, she's able to know what's going to happen. She can tell the future, because ... "It's already happened," she mutters.

Victor and Anton exchange a look as though she's gone crazy.

All this. It already happened. And so did the future. That's how I know about the evil forces. She looks at her boys, who are staring back at her earnestly. *But they don't know. They have no idea.*

She thinks for a moment, choosing her words. Her pledge to honesty extends to her boys as well. She decided a long time ago, back when they began to talk and understand things, that she didn't want to lie to them unless she absolutely had to. Even things that were difficult to handle became easier just by the fact that you could talk about them and didn't try to hide it.

The only big lie between them was the one about their father.

And she will tell them about that, in the near future.

But she can't tell them what's going to happen. That Victor will die.

So, Gina takes a breath. "Tell you what. We won't worry about what happened. For the rest of the day, we'll just have a good time. We'll be together, as a family. We'll do something fun. How's that?"

Both boys look hesitant at first, but when they realize she's serious, they light up like they used to do when they were little and Christmas rolled around.

"Well?" Gina asks. "Any ideas?"

"Bowling!" Anton says.

"Laser games!" Victor says.

Gina checks her watch. "If we hurry, we have time for both. But let's grab a burger first, shall we?"

"Awesome!" Victor says. "I'm starving."

They head for the restaurant the next block over. Anton begins chatting about other things, like what level he's at in his online game and what he did at recess. It's kind of unusual—

and it's not what happened

—because Anton was never the chatty one. Instead, right now, it's Victor taking the quieter role, walking next to Gina, looking down at his feet.

"A penny for your thoughts, Vic," Gina says.

He looks up at her. Then smiles. "I was just thinking, I'm proud of you, Mom."

The words make her stop dead in her tracks. Victor stops too. Anton doesn't notice, and just keeps walking.

He looks up at her, closing one eye because the sun is blinding him. He smiles. "Everything you've gone through. You did so well."

"Thank you, honey. I did my best."

He sighs, still smiling. "It's gonna be a fun day. I wish it never had to end."

Gina feels tears forming in her eyes. "Yeah, me too."

Victor's expression turns solemn. "But it already has ended, hasn't it?"

"I guess so."

Victor considers it briefly. "But then again, who's to say we can't make it last forever?"

When Anton finally realizes they've stopped, he turns and looks back. "Hey! You guys coming or what?"

Victor nods towards his brother. "I'm glad you didn't tell him. He doesn't need to know."

Gina pulls him into a tight hug, and she can no longer keep back the tears. She wants this day to last forever too. Wants desperately to hold on to Vic and never let go again.

"You shouldn't be afraid of anything bad happening, Mom," he whispers. "You just need to know what to do if it does."

"Mom?"

Anton's voice. Not coming from behind her, but from somewhere above.

The dream gradually dissipates, and Gina wakes up.

Blinking her eyes open, she sees Anton's face hovering above her. His expression is a perfect mixture of hope and anxiety. "Are you awake, Mom?"

Gina tries to tell him yes, but she can't find her voice. Instead, she gives a little nod and blinks.

Anton lets out a trembling breath. "You're really awake? Seriously?"

Seriously, Gina thinks, nodding again.

They're indoors somewhere. A soft daylight is coming in through a window.

"Oh, Mom!" He all but throws himself over her, hugging her fiercely. "I'm so glad you're back! John kept saying you'd come to, but I was really worried. He said it's normal to sleep for days after that kind of trauma, but I …" Anton stops himself. "I'm going to tell the others. Be right back." He rushes out of the room.

Gina just lies there, taking in the surroundings. The bed is very comfortable. The front end has been elevated slightly.

*Is this … a **hospice**?*

Looking at the windows, she sees a big, green lawn and a flower bed. The grass needs trimming. A couple of male blackbirds are fighting each other.

She becomes aware of a strange sensation in her right hand. She tries to lift it and finds that she barely has the strength. She manages to get it just above the blanket, and she's surprised to find her hand missing. Instead, she sees a white bandage wrapped around her arm.

Huh. So that really happened.

She suspects everything else did too, even though it all feels like a nightmare from a distant past. Maybe it's just the curious dream she just had that's messed up her sense of time.

Anton comes back into the room. His eyes go immediately to Gina's face. "Oh, good. You're still awake." He turns and waves eagerly. "Come on!"

Into the room comes Lisa, Nora, Alicia, and John, who's wearing both arms in slings. Then comes Mark, who's seated in a wheelchair. He's smiling. "Great to see you, Gina." Camilla comes next, cradling Danny on her arm. The boy looks noticeably older than the last time Gina saw him. Rex is there too, and he comes to lick her one remaining hand.

"How long …?" Gina croaks, pleasantly surprised to hear her own voice—though it's so raspy, it barely sounds like her.

"It's been six days," Anton answers immediately. Speaking of looking older, her son seems to have grown several inches. He looks more like a grown-up than a kid.

"You remember what happened?" Mark asks.

Gina thinks for a moment. "Most of it."

"We killed it, Mom," Anton says, beaming at her. "We stopped the monster. It changed everything. The hangar has been completely cleared out. All the people who stayed there are gone. We went to check." He throws out his arms. "They're no longer coming to kill us. And all the blind people have pretty much died by now."

"At least that's what we assume," John interjects with his usual, sober tone of voice. "It's still early on, but it seems like Anton could be right. It appears that now that Fritz and the monster are both gone, some kind of spell has been broken."

"Fritz too?" Gina whispers.

"Uh-huh," Anton says. "Camilla shot him."

Camilla doesn't exactly look as proud as Anton at the notion, but she gives a brief nod of confirmation.

Gina scans their faces, realizing they're one short. "Nick?"

For once, Anton isn't eager to answer. Instead, he looks over at Nora. The young woman takes a deep breath, then says, "He was killed. The monster got him."

"So sorry."

And then she remembers it. Seeing Nick die. She remembers hesitating. When John first charged the creature, he managed—incredibly—to keep it in an armbar for a few seconds. Gina could have shot it then. Unloaded the entire magazine in it. She would have probably killed it. But she would undoubtedly have killed John too. That's why she wavered. And because of it, John is alive, but instead, Nick is dead.

A life for a life. Another death she'll bear on her conscience until her dying days.

It was only when the monster was about to kill Nora too that Gina finally decided to take the chance and start firing. Luckily, she didn't hit Nora. And she takes comfort in knowing that Nick would love her for saving his sister's life—even if it was at the expense of his own.

"John broke his other arm," Mark adds. "Nora got some pretty mean bruises. I won't be playing soccer anytime soon, and you ..." He points at the bandages on Gina's arm. "You'll need to learn to wipe your butt with your left hand. Other than that, we're all fine!"

They all chuckle.

Then Gina asks, "Ghosts?"

"Gone," Anton says simply. "The sky is no longer broken, Mom. Even those of us who aren't immune, we can look at it just fine. And you know what the best thing is? It's happening all over the world. Check this out ..." He pulls out his phone, finds a picture and holds it in front of her.

It's a pretty gruesome shot taken back at the beach. It shows the monster, lying on its side, its head blown open, dark blood and greyish brain matter staining the sand.

"Jesus," Gina mutters as she's suddenly thrown back into the memory of that horrible, fateful night. She hears gunshots, hears screams and fire, and she hears the monster's voice.

"You never stood a chance, Gina."

"Maybe give your mom a little space, Anton," Camilla suggests. "It might be a bit much to take in."

"Oh, right, sorry," Anton mutters, taking the phone away. "It's just that, I posted this photo online. And it's gone completely viral. I mean, it's *everywhere*. You see, Mom, it's proof that the monsters can be killed. And it made other groups around the globe do the same." Anton is so excited, he can barely contain himself. "They're killing them, Mom. And then they put it online. Number five just came up this morning. In Brazil. It was a female; some of them are. Isn't it amazing?"

Gina nods. "It's great news."

"I think we were lucky," John interjects. "The creature we killed wasn't fully mature yet. Judging by the other killings, some of the monsters were even bigger and stronger. They were a lot harder to take down. Thousands of brave people have lost their lives already, and more will surely follow. There are still a lot of the creatures out there."

"But the resistance is getting smarter too," Anton says. "They're not just facing them head-on like we did. The one in Brazil, they trapped it somewhere, then drove it over with a truck. Crushed its skull. And this other one, I think it was in China, they blew up the building it was hiding in, so the whole thing came down over it. They found it in the rubble, all smashed up."

Gina looks at Anton. She can barely recognize him. He must still be burdened by the grief of his brother, but he's obviously dealt with the worst of it, and is able to function again. It makes her very proud.

"Who saved me?" she asks.

Anton beams. "I did. John guided me. Good thing we had all the emergency things ready."

"Thank you," Gina whispers, looking from her son to John. "Thank you both."

John smiles—which Gina has rarely seen him do, and Anton takes her hand and squeezes it. A moment of silence passes through the room.

"I'm pretty thirsty," Gina says.

"Of course," Nora says. "Let me get you some juice. You want something to eat too?"

"Yes, please."

"I think we should let Gina rest," John says, and Gina is thankful for the suggestion. She's very happy to see them all, but she's also very tired. As soon as she has eaten, she'll no doubt go back to sleep.

"I'll go too," Anton tells her, after the others have left. "But I'll be close by, so you can just call me if you need anything. Okay?"

"Okay. Thanks, honey."

Anton bends over and kisses her forehead. "I love you, Mom."

"Love you too."

He leaves the door ajar.

Gina is once again alone in the silence.

She can't help but go back there once more. To the beach. She recalls what the monster told her. About how it'll rise again no matter what they do.

That may be true. But then again, what was it Victor told her in the dream?

Victor.

The thought of him makes her heart hurt. He's really gone.

"You shouldn't be afraid of anything bad happening, Mom," her son whispers in her memory. "*You just need to know what to do if it does.*"

Gina looks out the window again, and she smiles as a tear rolls down her cheek.

Strangely, the dream seems to have left some profound peace inside of her. It was like a sign from a deeper intelligence inside of her. A promise that while the world is still in chaos, it's not broken. And that the future is still possible.

But not only that.

The most important message from the dream was about her son.

A reassurance that Victor is safe and surrounded by love.

Wherever he is.

THANK YOU

I can't believe it's over.

Back in 2020, when I set out to write this series, I had no idea where it would go or how it would end up. I did know, however, that it would be the biggest and longest series I'd ever written. That much came true. Not much else about this story I could have foreseen.

I knew I wanted a strong, female lead. I've never really done one before, and I've read far too few stories about them. Whenever they do appear, they often act like men with wigs, kicking other men's asses. That's not the strength I wanted Gina to have. I wanted her to be courageous and dangerous, but most of all, love should be her source of power. On the surface, muscles and guns may rule the world, but if you look closer, I believe a mother's love is much more powerful. It can make or break anyone. It even can—and probably someday will—determine the fate of mankind. I guess that became the underlying message of this story—even though I'm very careful with those, because I don't like fiction that's too preachy.

There are a couple of other characters I wanted to comment on briefly: Mark and Tommy. Along with Gina, I consider them the Three Originals. I really didn't expect them all to make it to the end. My money was on Mark to cave first. I felt sure he was on a collision course, but to my surprise, he managed to turn things around. I've heard from a lot of readers who disliked him at first, then grew to love him. I didn't set out to make him dislikable, I just thought the whole cheating thing was an interesting flaw to explore. I identify deeply with all my characters, and Mark is no different. I never crossed the lines he did, but I understood what drove him to do it. I knew right away that his reckless, detached attitude was really him running scared of commitment.

Tommy is probably the most tragic character I've ever written. In a way, his story is darker than some of the grimmer characters in the story—like Thorn or Fritz, to name a couple—because unlike those guys, Tommy actually had the chance to save himself—he just didn't take it. This was also a surprise to me. I knew from the onset he was an intelligent guy, and I thought for sure he was going to figure it out. In fact, I figured he would become the brains of the survivor group, because of his love of science. It broke my heart every time he took another step down deeper into the darkness, until it was clear he was never getting back out again. I'm glad he got a somewhat happy ending, though. Or at least a little redemption.

Anyway, I'm thrilled you made it to the end with me. That truly means a lot. I know not all readers did. While this series is probably my most popular, as it went along, it also became harder to pin down. It's definitely blending genres, and it pulls in elements I hadn't expected. I'm sure it wasn't everyone's cup of tea. I felt I had no other choice than to go where it led me. So, you being here, reading this, at the very least means you wanted to know how it all ended.

And on that note, I hope you're satisfied. I know I am. Or, more accurately, I'm drained. Having this huge story with all its many characters pass through me and get turned into words was both a privilege and a huge effort. I'll probably go take a long nap now.

One last thing. If you haven't read the free prequel, *Blind Gods*, you can still get it as soon as you join my newsletter at **nick-clausen.com/blind-gods**. It tells the story of what happened six years prior to the crack in the sky. My newsletters is also the best way to get in touch with me and stay in the loop. If you feel like shooting me an email and telling me what you thought of the ending, please don't hold back. There are few things I love more than hearing from people who've read my books.

So ... where do we go now?

I'm always trying to make the next story my best story. I have no idea what the future brings, because I don't (can't) plan anything. But I promise you this: I'll never stop writing.

Until then, I have a few other series you might want to check out. You'll find them all on my website, **nick-clausen.com**.

Thanks again for reading. Hope we'll meet again soon.

—Nick

Printed in Great Britain
by Amazon